I0595308

George Reber

**Therapentae St. John Never in Asia Minor**

George Reber

**Therapentae St. John Never in Asia Minor**

ISBN/EAN: 9783337315467

Printed in Europe, USA, Canada, Australia, Japan

Cover: Foto ©Andreas Hilbeck / pixelio.de

More available books at **www.hansebooks.com**

# ST. JOHN NEVER IN ASIA MINOR.

## IRENÆUS,
### THE AUTHOR OF THE FOURTH GOSPEL.

### THE FRAUDS OF THE CHURCHMEN OF THE SECOND CENTURY EXPOSED.

PUBLISHED BY THE AUTHOR,
GEORGE REBER.

Entered according to Act of Congress in the year 1872, by
GEORGE REBER,
In the office of the Librarian of Congress at Washington.

POOLE & MACLAUCHLAN,
PRINTERS AND BOOKBINDERS,
205-213 *East 12th St.*

# ERRATA.

On page 84, 4th line.  It should read : *for almost twenty centuries.*

On page 100, 12th line.  It should read : Victor was Bishop of Rome in the beginning of the *third* century.

On page 140, 19th line, the figures 55 should be *65.*

On page 170, 3d line.  It should read : *the omission of the first two chapters of Matthew.*

On page 235, 7th line.  It should read : The Epistle of Jude is nothing but a bolt hurled at the head of *Paul.*

# CONTENTS.

## CHAPTER VII.



## CHAPTER VIII.



## CHAPTER IX.



## CHAPTER X.



## CHAPTER XI.



## CHAPTER XII.

## CHAPTER XIII.



## CHAPTER XIV.



## CHAPTER XV.



## CHAPTER XVI.



## CHAPTER XVII.



## CHAPTER XVIII.

## CHAPTER XIX.



## CHAPTER XX.



## CHAPTER XXI.



## CHAPTER XXII.



## CHAPTER XXIII.



## CHAPTER XXIV.



## CHAPTER XXV.

# THERAPEUTÆ.

## CHAPTER I.

Death of Stephen.—Conversion of Paul.—His retirement to Arabia and return to Damascus and Jerusalem.

LET the reader imagine that he is in Jerusalem, in Judea, about the year A.D. 34. There is unusual tumult in the vicinity of the Temple. A large crowd has gathered, and, stirred up by some strong provocation, is swayed like the billows in a storm. As we approach, we see a young man, who is trying to raise his voice above the din. There is something very striking in his looks. He is pale, but firm. His eyes gleam with an unearthly light. As the crowd surges and threatens, he is calm. His thoughts and looks are directed more to Heaven than Earth.

But in this crowd there is a young man of

1*

an entirely different stamp. He is excited and angry. His eyes are red with rage, and he is seen moving among the crowd like an incendiary. The crisis came, and poor Stephen stood first on the list of Christian martyrs. This little bleared-eyed, angry man is not yet satisfied. Like the tiger that has tasted blood, he thirsts for more. He goes about Jerusalem like a madman. He fills the prisons with men and women who believed with Stephen. When he had done all the injury he could in Jerusalem, he asked and received permission to go to Damascus on a like mission. On his way, while he is breathing out threatenings and slaughter, he is struck down in his mad career. He saw in it the hand of God. Everything is changed in a moment. The fiery stream of burning lava, which rushed in one direction, now turned and ran with equal violence the other way.

Philosophers may differ as to what befell Paul on his way to Damascus; but as for himself, he never doubted. The Christ that he persecuted had spoken to him. His faith in what he saw in his vision he bore in his bosom, as he did his heart; and in a life of toil, suffering, and sorrow, he clung to it to the end.

We can hardly tell what were the feelings of Paul when he awoke to consciousness, because we cannot judge him as we would other men. He had raised his hand against the Son of God, and now, after a severe reproof, he was appointed by him to be his special minister on earth. Paul did do just what we might suppose he would. He withdrew from the world, avoided Jerusalem, and, as he says, went into Arabia. There, alone, he meditated over the wonderful scenes through which he had passed. The more he thought, the more he believed he had talked with Christ, the Son of God, and the more he believed he had been selected to spread his Gospel throughout the earth.

Once convinced that his vision was a reality, it was natural for him to make himself believe that these visions were repeated; and through life, in all his acts and movements, he believed he was under the guidance of the same hand that smote him on the plains of Damascus. He goes from place to place as a Spirit from above directs him, and when he speaks he speaks not for himself, but for Him who sent him. Positive and overbearing by nature, he imagines himself to be the minister of the Son of God, and becomes intolerant, vain and exacting. All his ideas are crystallized—and will not bend or yield.

As he was specially selected to preach, he believed in the doctrine of election. When he believed at all, he believed too much; for it was his nature to overrun. He had witnessed Christ—others had not; but, in the absence of proof, they must substitute faith. Works are nothing—faith everything. What he saw and believed, others must believe without seeing.

His theology, from his natural temperament and the circumstances of his conversion, took an austere cast, which made the relation between man and the Creator, that of guardian and ward. God himself, in the mind of Paul, is almost hideous. Some are given over to damnation before they are born; while others are destined to be saved before they have had a chance to sin.

It is difficult to tell whether the religious faith of Paul was fully fixed and determined before he left his retreat in Arabia and returned to Damascus, or whether it was the growth of after experience and reflection. At some period of his life, and early too, he had settled in his mind the true relation which Christ bore to humanity. He had the best of reasons for his belief on that subject. He was in Jerusalem at a time when it was not impossible that Mary herself was living; and if not, he saw Peter and was with him fifteen days, when he had every opportunity to inform himself about the early history of Christ. Will any one say that Paul, with a mind awake to everything that related to Christ, would not inquire and find out all that was known about Him who had spoken to him from the clouds, when he was in Jerusalem, and could question those who had been his companions on this earth? If there was anything remarkable about his birth or death, Peter would have told it, and Paul would have repeated it all along the shores of the Archipelago, or wherever he went.

But Paul, from first to last, preached that Christ was born of woman, and was of the seed of Abraham according to the flesh. Upon this point he yielded nothing, and stood to it to the death. Paul was a man of learning, and wrote with great power. Longinus classed him among the great men of Greece. But in action and in deeds is where he went beyond all other men. Upon his shoulders, as he believed, was left the conversion of the world; and he had a will and energy equal to the task. Believing that the Son of God stood at his side, as he performed the mission which had been assigned him, he neither feared nor trembled, but stood up with a bold front in the presence of Festus and King Agrippa. The unsparing cruelty of Nero had no terrors for him.

After Paul had remained in Arabia long enough to collect his thoughts, and determine the course he should pursue, he went back to Damascus. At last he made up his mind to go to Jerusalem and see Peter. What must have been his feelings as he approached the holy city, and passed along the place where he assisted, three years before, in the death of Stephen! Paul never forgave himself for the part he took in this murder

Can we imagine with what feelings he approached Peter, or why he approached him at all? If he felt sad and grieved at the part he took in the death of Stephen, he did not feel as if he met Peter as his superior, for he conceded nothing to any of the Apostles. There was no point upon which he was more sensitive. Paul did not visit Peter to be taught and instructed as to his duties, nor to learn from him the great truths of Christianity; for he had learned all this from a higher source, and felt himself more able to give instruction than to receive it from others. Speaking of his doctrines, he says : " For I neither received it of man, neither was I taught it, but by the revelation of Jesus Christ" (*Galatians* i. 12). Doubtless he came to learn from Peter everything he knew of the personal history of Christ. He had many questions to ask about his habits—mode of life—his employments—about Mary, Joseph, and the whole family of Jesus. The smallest incident in his early life would be dear to Paul, and he would lock the remembrance of it in his bosom, as a sacred treasure.

In this way fifteen days passed over, when Paul again left Jerusalem, and afterwards went

into Syria and Cilicia, where he was followed
by divine visions and revelations.   He spent the
year A.D. 42 in Antioch, where he taught, assisted by Barnabas.   Here he took up a collec-
tion for the brethren of Judea, who were suffering from the effects of a famine which took place
during the reign of Claudius Cæsar, and returned with it to Jerusalem.   Having discharged his trust, he went back to Antioch, accom-
panied by Barnabas and Mark.   All we know
with certainty about Paul, from this time forward, we must gather, for the most part, from
his Epistles to the churches;   for all other
sources of information are suspicious and doubtful.   An act, especially one of importance connected with his labors as an Apostle, attributed
to him by others, and not spoken of at all by
himself, should be excluded from the pages of
authentic history.

# CHAPTER II.

Paul and Barnabas start west to preach the Gospel.—
The prevailing ideas on religion in Asia Minor.
—Theology of Plato and Philo.—The effect pro-
duced by the preaching of Paul.

PAUL, in the year A.D. 45, with Barnabas
and Mark as his companions, set his face west
in the direction of Asia Minor. The people
who inhabited the country from Antioch in
Syria along the north coast of the Mediterranean and the Ægean, or the Archipelago, to
Thessalonica in Macedonia, were for the most
part descendants of the early colonists from
Greece. A large number of cities were scattered along the shores, which had been enriched
by commerce, and were the seats of learning
and luxury. The Greek of Asia Minor, in the
latter part of the first century, was not the
Greek of the time of Pericles and Epaminondas.

His levity and cunning had outlived his courage, his love of country and stern endurance. The college at Alexandria was the source of all light and learning, and the doctrines of that celebrated school, like a subtle fluid, pervaded all classes of men. It was here that Plato took lessons which led him to explore the mysterious nature of the Deity, and expose to the eyes of mortals the nature of the divine persons who regulated the affairs of the universe. In his imagination he populated Heaven, and divided among the different deities the share of each in the government of the world. According to Plato there was one God who was superessential, and in him was blended or united all that was powerful and good. This he called the *One*, or the first principle of things. Proculus, of the same school, says the *One* is the God of all gods, the Unity of the unities, the Holy among the holies. Plato compares him with the sun. For as the sun by his light not only confers the power of being seen on visible objects, but is likewise the cause of their generation, nutriment, and increase, so the good of the One, through superessential light, imparts being and power. As a consequence, both Plato and Pythagoras conclude that the immediate issue of this ineffable Cause must be gods, and each must partake of the same nature and have a superessential existence. That " everything in nature which is the result of progression exists in a mysterious unity and similitude with its first cause. They are superessential, and differ in no respect from the highest good. From the supereminent Cause, as from an exalted place of survey, we may contemplate the divine unities, that is, the gods, flowing in admirable and ineffable order, and at the same time abiding in profound union with each other, and with their Cause."

The first procession, from the first *One*, or intelligible Cause, is the intelligible *Triad*, consisting of *Being*, *Life*, and *Intellect*, which are the three highest things after the first God. Plato, in his *Parmenides*, calls the Author of the Universe *Intellect* and *Father*, and represents him commanding the junior gods to imitate the power which he employed in their generation. It follows, that that which generated from the Father is offspring, Son or Logos, second in the Triad. The third power or principle in the Triad is *Intellect*, or Spirit of the Universe. Here we have the *Father*, the *Logos*, and the Soul of the Universe in a mysterious union; and as they all proceed from the *One*, are one in unity. The author of "Decline and Fall" thus defines the theology of Plato: "The vain hope of extricating himself from these difficulties which must forever oppress the feeble powers of the human mind, might induce Plato to consider the divine nature under the threefold modification of the *First Cause*, the Reason or Logos and the *Soul* or Spirit of the Universe. His poetical imagination sometimes fixed and animated these metaphysical abstractions; the three archial or original principles were represented in the Platonic system as three gods, united with each other by a mysterious and ineffable generation; and the Logos was particularly considered, under the more accessible character of the Son of an Eternal Father, and the Creator and Governor of the world." (Vol. I., page 438.)

Such is an outline of the theology of Plato, as we learn it from the "Explanatory translation" of Taylor to the *Cratylus* and other works of the great light of Greece. The ideas of Plato, under the teachings of the Alexandrian school, underwent changes and modifications, but were the source of all subsequent systems of theology, and we can readily detect in each the genius of the Athenian. Through the invitation of the Ptolemies, large numbers of Jews settled in the new capital of Egypt, who carried with them the laws and institutions of Moses. It was not many years before the religious ideas of the descendants of the colonists were tinctured and in some degree moulded after the doctrines taught at the school of Alexandria. Under the lead of Philo a new school arose, which was formed from a union of " Mosaic faith and Grecian philosophy," in which the distinctive features of each are clearly preserved.

Philo Judæus was an Alexandrian Jew, descended from a noble and sacerdotal family, and was distinguished in his day for his wisdom and eloquence. He was born before Christ, and survived him. He was the author of numerous works, and esteemed one of the most learned men of his day. A tumult arose in

Alexandria between the Jews and the Greeks, and out of each party three were chosen as embassadors to go to Rome and lay the case before Caligula, who was then emperor. Philo was chosen as one to represent his countrymen, and undertook to act as chief spokesman in the imperial presence. He was treated with insolence—ordered to be silent—and the emperor was so carried away by his passions that personal violence seemed imminent. The equanimity of the philosopher was not disturbed, and having discharged his duty, he quitted the palace filled with the contempt for the tyrant which has loaded his memory in all subsequent ages. (Josephus, *Antiq.*, lib. xviii. ch. 8, sec. 1.)

The system taught by Philo dispensed with the third person in the Godhead, which was composed of the Father and the *Logos*, a divine *Duad*, which did not exist in unity, like the trinity of Plato: but the *Logos* with him, like the Mediator of the Hebrews, was possessed of mediatorial powers, and was an intercessor in behalf of the fallen race of Adam. It is difficult to define the relation of the *Logos* of Philo with the Creator of the Universe, whether he is an attribute which is made manifest in creative power, or whether he has a separate existence. He is the Son of God, and was with the Father before the world was created. His powers embrace the mediatorial, and he stands between God and man, and represents the Father in his providences to our race. He is not an hypostasis, and yet he was begotten.

Such are some of the ideas which prevailed in Asia Minor, and other countries along the shores of the Mediterranean, when Paul and Barnabas entered the country, bringing with them a new religion.. It is as difficult to define what Paul's real belief was of the relations which Christ bore to the Creator, as it is to determine the real belief of Philo on the same subject. With Paul, Christ was the Son of God, but what was the exact relation he did not pretend to say. He says he is less than the angels—superior to Moses (*Hebrews* ii. and iii.) ; but he nowhere says he is equal to God. Paul seems to have been less concerned about the nature of Christ, and the place occupied by him in the Godhead, than he was about his mediatorial powers. Through the fall of Adam, all men were under condemnation, and it was the office of Christ, through his blood, to make atonement, and once more restore man to the favor of the Creator. With him Christ was not the Creator, like the *Logos* of Philo, but was the Saviour of the world. He did not exist from the beginning, but, like all flesh, from his natural birth. But still he was, as was the *Logos* of Philo, the Son of God.

With such ideas, Paul made his way among the Greeks. The Jews were the first to make war upon him. But he stood his ground and gained more. The small churches which he established were like so many fortresses in an enemy's country. Wherever he went he started discussion. The friction between the new and the old ideas produced heat : and with heat came light.

But, after all, Paul's converts, for the most part, were from the less informed and the middle classes. The learned turned away from him, because he had no tangible proof to satisfy them that what he preached was true. The story of his conversion was improbable, and could be ascribed to the effects of natural causes.

The time for miracles had not yet come, and Paul did not claim anything from them.*

Tacitus speaks of Christians as a race of men detested for their evil practices, and classes their doctrines among the pernicious things which flowed into Rome as into a common sewer. (*Annals*, lib. xv. sec 54.) Still the churches established by Paul grew slowly, but seemed to require the influence of his presence and personal efforts to keep them alive. As long as the fight went on between Paul and the Jews, and unconverted Gentiles, his lofty courage and iron will were enough to hold him up. But he soon had troubles of a different kind. He found them in the churches themselves. It is not difficult to tell what would be the effect of Paul's ideas when brought face to face with doctrines of the Alexandrian school. It was like the meeting of the acid and the alkali. The first sign of the effervescence appears at Corinth, and two hundred years passed before it ceased, if it ceased at all. From the time the quarrel commenced at Co-

---

* Had it been true that an apron which came in contact with Paul's person could cure diseases, all Asia would have been converted while he was making a few hundred believers.

rinth, between the followers of Paul, until the time when the questions disappear altogether, mental phenomena are exhibited unlike any other in the history of man. Even the quarrels and disputes of the Realists and Nominalists of the thirteenth century bear no comparison. The contest between the different sects had all the earnestness of a struggle between gladiators. From being warm disputants, men became dishonest. Books were forged entire, others were mutilated, and some suppressed and put out of sight. It was an age of downright dishonesty on all sides. But from these dark and discordant elements arose the true Church.

# CHAPTER III.

Therapeutæ of Philo—and Essenes of Josephus.—An account of them.—Their disappearance from history, and what became of them.

IN the beginning of the first century there existed a sect or society which exercised great influence over the fortune and affairs of the world; but, before the second had elapsed, was insensibly lost in the commingling of creeds and sects which sprang up in the mean time. Like a billow on the sea, it rose high and spread far; but at last disappears, or is lost in the great ocean. We refer to the Therapeutæ of Philo and the Essenes of Josephus. Their origin is lost in the distant past; nor is it proven who was the founder of the sect. Although the Therapeutæ were found in every part of the Roman empire, Alexandria was the centre of their operations. Their learning and knowledge were derived from the schools of Alexandria; and to the climate of Egypt, which, by some immuta-

ble law of nature, disposed men to embrace a
gloomy asceticism, they are indebted for their
morose and cruel discipline.   From this society
were furnished all the monks which populated
the deserts of Africa before the Christian era
began.

The Essenes were one of the three leading
sects among the Jews; the Sadducees and Pharisees forming the other two.   Josephus, who fully
describes them, in early life was a member, and
for three years took up his abode in the desert,
and suffered all the pains, and endured all the
hardships of monastic life.   They were confined
to no locality, but were found in every city in
Europe and Asia.   When travelling from place
to place, they were received and provided for
by members of their sect without charge, so
that when one of them made his appearance in
a strange city, he found there one already appointed for the special purpose of taking care of
strangers and providing for their wants.   They
neither bought from nor sold to each other, but
each took what his wants required, as if it were
his own.

" And as for their piety towards God," says

Josephus, " it is very extraordinary; for before
sun-rising they speak not a word about profane
matters, but put up certain prayers which they
have received from their forefathers, as if they
made a supplication for its rising. After this,
every one of them is sent away by their curators,
to exercise some of those arts wherein they are
skilled, in which they labor with great diligence
till the fifth hour, after which they assemble
themselves together in one place, and when
they have clothed themselves in white veils,
they then bathe their bodies in cold water, and,
after their purification is over, they every one
meet together in an apartment of their own,
into which it is not permitted to any of another
sect to enter; while they go after a pure manner
into the dining-room, as into a certain holy temple, and quietly sit themselves down; upon
which the baker lays their loaves in order; the
cook also brings a single plate of one sort of
food and sets it before every one of them; but
a priest says grace before meat; and it is unlawful for any one to taste of the food before
grace be said. The same priest, when he has
dined, says grace again after meat; and when

they begin, and when they end, they praise
God, as he that bestows their food upon them ;
after which they lay aside their [white] garments, and betake themselves to their labors
again until the evening ; then they return home
to supper, after the same manner." (Josephus,
*Wars*, lib. ii. chap. 8, sec. 5.)

The time allowed for probation, before admission to the fraternity, was three years, and in
the mean time the temper and disposition of the
neophyte were put to the severest test, and not
until he had given ample proof of his sincerity
or ability to submit to the laws and ordinances
of the sect was he deemed fit for admission ;
but before he is allowed to do so, he is required
to swear, " that, in the first place, he will exercise piety towards God ; and then that he will
observe justice towards men ; and that he will
do no harm to any one, either of his own accord,
or by the command of others ; that he will always hate the wicked, and be assistant to the
righteous ; that he will ever show fidelity to all
men, and especially to those in authority, because no one obtains the government without
God's assistance ; and that if he be in authority,

he will at no time whatever abuse his authority, nor endeavor to outshine his subjects, either in his garments, or any other finery; that he will be perpetually a lover of truth, and propose to himself to reprove those that tell lies; and that he will keep his hands clear from theft, and his soul from unlawful gains; and that he will neither conceal anything from those of his own sect, nor discover any of their doctrines to others—no, not though any one should compel him so to do, at the hazard of his life. Moreover, he swears to communicate their doctrines to no one any otherwise than as he received them himself; that he will abstain from robbery, and will equally preserve their books belonging to their sect, and the names of the angels [or messengers]. These are the oaths by which they secure their proselytes to themselves." (Jos., *Wars,* lib. ii. ch. 8, sec. 6.)

The following is the account given by Philo of this sect, preserved in the pages of Eusebius :—

" ' This kind of men is everywhere scattered over the world, for the Greeks and barbarians should share in so permanent a benefit. They

abound, however, in Egypt, in each of its dis-
tricts, and particularly Alexandria. But the
principal men among them from every quarter
emigrate to a place situated on a moderate
elevation of land beyond the Lake Maria, very
advantageously located both for safety and
temperature of the air, as if it were the native
country of the Therapeutæ.'"

"After describing what kind of habitations
they have, he says of the churches : ' In every
house there is a sacred apartment which they
call the Semneion or Monasterium, where,
retired from men, they perform the mysteries
of a pious life. Hither they bring nothing
with them, neither drink nor food, nor anything
else requisite to the necessities of the body ;
they only bring the law and the inspired declarations of the prophets, and hymns, and such
things by which knowledge and piety may be
augmented and perfected.' After other matters
he adds : ' The whole time between the morning
and the evening is a constant exercise ; for as they
are engaged with the sacred Scriptures, they reason and comment upon them, explaining the philosophy of their country in an allegorical manner.

For they consider the verbal interpretation as signs indicative of a sacred sense communicated in obscure intimations. They have also commentaries of ancient men, who, as founders of the sect, have left many monuments of their doctrine in allegorical representations which they use as certain models, imitating the manner of the original institution.'

" These facts appear to have been stated by a man who at least has paid attention to those that have expounded the sacred writings. But it is highly probable that the ancient commentaries which he says they have are the very Gospels and writings of the Apostles, and probably some expositions of the ancient prophets, such as are contained in the Epistle to the Hebrews, and many others of St. Paul's epistles. Afterwards again, concerning the new psalms which they composed, he thus writes : ' Thus they not only pass their time in meditation, but compose songs and hymns unto God, noting them of necessity with measure uncommonly serious through every variety of metres and tunes.' Many other things concerning these persons, he writes in the same book . . .

Why need we add to these an account of their meet
ings, and the separate abodes of the men and
the women in these meetings, and the exercises
performed by them, which are still in vogue
among us at the present day, and which, especially at the festival of our Saviour's passion, we
are accustomed to use in our fastings and
watchings, and in the study of the divine word.
All these the above-mentioned author has accurately described and stated in his writings,
and they are the same customs that are observed
by us alone at the present day, particularly the
vigils of the great festival, and the exercises in
them, and the hymns that are commonly recited
among us. He states that whilst one sings
gracefully with a certain measure, the others,
listening in silence, join in singing the final
clauses of the hymns ; also, that on the above-
mentioned days they lie on straw spread on
the ground, and to use his own words, ' They
abstain altogether from wine, and taste no flesh.
Water is their only drink, and the relish of their
bread, salt and hyssop.' Besides this, he describes the grades of dignity among those who
administer the ecclesiastical services committed

to them, those of the *Deacons* and the *Presiden-cies* of the *Episcopate* as the highest. But, whosoever desires to have a more accurate knowledge of these things, may learn them from the history already cited ; but that Philo, when he wrote these statements, had in view the first heralds of the gospel, and the original practices handed down from the Apostles, must be obvious to all." (Euseb. *Ecc. Hist.*, lib. ii. ch. 17.)

They had their churches, their Bishops (called Presidencies of the Episcopate), Deacons and monasteries. They used sacred writings, which they read in their churches with comments, and which they believed were divinely inspired. Commentaries were written on these writings, as they are on the present Gospels. Their mode of worship was much the same as in our own day; and they had missionaries all over Asia, and in many parts of Europe. The day observed by Christians afterwards as the festival of our Saviour's passion was observed by them as sacred, and which they passed in fasting, watching, and the study of the sacred writings. All this we are assured is true, by the authority of Josephus, Philo,

and Eusebius.  So strong is the resemblance
in doctrines, and form of church government,
between these ancient Therapeutæ, that Eusebius, because he could not deny the similitude,
undertook the task of proving that the Essenes
were Christians, and that their sacred writings
were the four Gospels.  He says: "But it
is highly probable that the ancient writings
which he (Philo) says they have, are the very
Gospels and writings of the Apostles, and probably some expositions of the ancient prophets,
such as are contained in the Epistle to the
Hebrews, and many others of St. Paul's epistles."  (Eus., *Ecc. Hist.*, lib. ii. ch. 17.)

Eusebius has not deceived himself—he only
hoped to deceive others.  If the Essenes were
not Christians, then it is evident that much
which is claimed as original in Christianity was
copied from them.  "Basnage has examined
with the most critical accuracy the curious
treatise of Philo, which describes the Therapeutæ.  By proving that it was composed as
early as the time of Augustus, he has demonstrated, in spite of Eusebius and a crowd of
*modern Catholics*, that the Therapeutæ were

neither Christians nor monks." (*Decline and Fall*, Vol. I. page 283, chapter xv., note 162.)

"Much dispute has arisen among the learned concerning this sect. Some have imagined them to be Judaizing Gentiles; but Philo supposes them to be Jews, by speaking of them as a branch of the sect of the Essenes, and especially classes them among the followers of Moses. Others have maintained that the Therapeutæ were an Alexandrian sect of Jewish converts to the Christian faith, who devoted themselves to monastic life. But this is impossible, for Philo, who wrote before Christianity appeared in Egypt, speaks of this as an established fact." (Buck's *Theological Dictionary.*)

And now, what has become of the Therapeutæ?—of their sacred writings? Where are their Elders, their Deacons and the Presidency of the Episcopate, or Bishops? All writers agree that they soon disappeared after the introduction of Christianity. "How long," continues Buck, "this sect continued, is uncertain, but it is not improbable that after the appearance of Christianity in Egypt, it soon became extinct." Gibbon, in speaking of the disappearance of this sect from history, says : " It still remains probable that they changed their names, preserved their manners, and adopted some new article of faith." (Vol. I. page 283, n. 162.)

This sect did not mingle and lose itself in the huge mass of Pagans, for between the two there was no neutral ground on which they might meet and agree. The antagonism between them had continued too long, and there was traditional hatred on both sides. Paul threw the doors of the church wide open, and, as we shall see, the Therapeutæ soon entered, and by their numbers took possession, and barred them against the founder and all his followers. What did the Therapeutæ do with their sacred writings, which, Eusebius claims, were nothing more than our present Gospels ? To suppose that they abandoned and destroyed them altogether is not possible, considering their antiquity, and the veneration in which they were held for generations.

# CHAPTER IV.

### THE ORIGIN OF THE CHURCH.

IT is a question of great interest in history, if nothing more, when and where it was that the Christian Church, in the form in which it has come down to us, had its origin.

To be sure, there are many who are satisfied with an orthodox belief on the subject, because they have never questioned their sources of information. But the world has grown to that age when traditional dogmas, or whatever they may be called, must be subject to the test which advancing knowledge imposes. Tried by this test, what is true will appear brighter ; what is false will be thrown off ; and man, relieved of a burden which only weighed him down, will move on to an improved and better life. Man is not doomed by the condition of his nature to be eternally tugging at the stone of Sisyphus— nor is it consistent with the laws of a wise and beneficent Creator that mankind, in order to be prosperous and happy, should be compelled to live under a perpetual delusion. Like the source of some river, often traced to a mountain rill or the oozing waters of a morass, so the beginning of the church or churches of our own day is to be looked for in some obscure corner of history, covered by the *debris* of ages.

Located on a narrow isthmus between the Ægean and Ionian seas stood Corinth, one of the principal cities of Greece. Situated where the commerce from the East and the West meet *in transitu*, it grew in opulence and wealth, and was distinguished for the arts, and for the luxury and licentiousness of its inhabitants. Here Venus had a temple, presided over by a thousand priestesses, whose attractions increased the numbers who came from all parts of Greece to assist in celebrating the Isthmian games. It was at this place Paul planted a church, between the years A.D. 51 and A.D. 53, and where he remained eighteen months, working as no one but himself could work to build up and strengthen it.

Paul left Corinth for a time for other fields

of labor, because he belonged to no one place, but his mission embraced the world. The commerce of Corinth attracted to the place people from every part of the empire, east and west, and with others a large number of Alexandrian Jews. Among them were many of the Therapeutæ, who brought with them into Greece the doctrines of Philo.

During Paul's absence there came to Corinth Apollos of Alexandria. He was an eloquent man and learned in the Scriptures. It is a subject of regret that we do not know more of his history than we find in the Acts, and in the Epistles of Paul. What were the doctrines he taught when he first appeared in Ephesus, where he spent some time before he went to Corinth, we cannot tell, but he was fervent in spirit, " and taught diligently the things of the Lord." He had heard of John the Baptist, for he was a historic character, and Josephus tells how he baptized multitudes in the waters of the Jordan ; but he seems to have known nothing about Christ or the doctrines he taught. He spoke in the synagogue, which proves that what he taught did not give offence to the Jews. In

Ephesus he attracted the notice of Aquila and Priscilla, Jewish Christians, who had been expelled from Rome by the Emperor Claudius on account of some disturbance growing out of quarrels between Jews and Christians.*  Under their instructions Apollos was made a convert to Christianity.

The Jews, as has been shown, were divided into three sects—Pharisees, Sadducees, and the Essenes.  Every Jew belonged to or connected himself with the one or the other.  Those who went to Alexandria, in time took the name of Therapeutæ, which, it is claimed, was the same as the Essenes.  However this may be, Philo describes them as a Jewish sect.  That Apollos was one of them may be claimed with great reason.  A Jew, born in Alexandria, he could scarcely escape being one.  Raised under the shadow of the college of Alexandria, of a fervent spirit and a man of thought, he could not fail to be impressed by the doctrines taught by that celebrated school.  They were the prevailing and fashionable doctrines of the day.  That he

---

* See Appendix A.

brought with him to Ephesus the Logos idea of Philo is clearly proven by what took place after his arrival. It seems his conversion to the Christian faith under the instruction of Aquila and Priscilla was easy, which proves that the difference which separated them in the first place was not great. Like all Jews, he was looking for some kind of Saviour or Deliverer, and they convinced him that Christ was , the one. He now undertook to convince others. " For he mightily convinced the Jews, and that publicly, shewing by the Scriptures that Jesus was Christ." (*Acts* xviii. 28.) But the Alexandrian notions of the Logos or Son of God soon began to show out in his discourses and make trouble. Some began to cry, I am for Paul; and others, I am for Apollos (1 *Cor.* iii. 4).

Paul's ideas on some points did not suit the Alexandrian school. The birth of Christ from human parents, in the speculative minds of this people, stripped him of all mystery ; and with them, on subjects like this, where there is no mystery there is nothing real. There could be no other difference between the followers of Paul and Apollos, except as to the origin and nature of Christ, and his relations to the Creator ; and thcre was none.  The strife grew to such dimensions that Paul is constrained to write an epistle to the church, in which we can see what was at the bottom of the trouble. In his First Epistle to the Corinthians, Paul names four parties whose quarrels disturbed the peace of the Church : the Paul party, who maintained the doctrines of Paul as to the human origin of Christ ; the party of Apollos, who, without doubt, taught the docrines of Philo ; the party of Cephas, which held to the doctrines of circumcision ; and the Christ party. We infer that the last was composed of negative men, or those who occupied neutral ground— the *fence* men of our day.  It could not have been of much importance, for we never hear of it again.

It was neither the first, third, or fourth of these parties that called out the letter to the Corinthians.  It was the wisdom of the Greek school and Apollos' " excellency of speech " that disturbed Paul, and continued to do so to the end of his life.  But see with what force he opposes the wisdom of the Greeks, the revelations which came to him from God. This letter displays all the characteristics of Paul. " And my speech and my preaching was not with enticing words of man's wisdom, but in demonstration of the Spirit, and of power : that your faith should not stand in the wisdom of men, but in the power of God. But God hath revealed *them* unto us by His Spirit ; for the Spirit searcheth all things, yea, the deep things of God. Now we have received, not the spirit of the world, but the Spirit which is of God ; that we might know the things that are freely given to us of God. Which things also we speak, not in the words which man's wisdom teacheth, but which the Holy Ghost teacheth ; comparing spiritual things with spiritual. But the natural man receiveth not the things of the Spirit of God : for they are foolishness unto him : neither can he know *them*, because they are spiritually discerned. But he that is spiritual judgeth all things, yet he himself is judged of no man. For who hath known the mind of the Lord, that he may instruct him ? But *we have the mind of Christ.*" (1 *Cor.* ch. ii.) Here it is not Paul that denounces the wisdom of the Greek school, but it is God himself. Such is Paul.

It is not difficult to tell to which of the four parties at Corinth this epistle was addressed. That the difference between Paul and Apollos grew out of opposing opinions as to the nature of Christ, can admit of no doubt, which is rendered certain by the first, second, and third chapters of his First Epistle to the Corinthians. He says: " For other foundation can no man lay than *that is laid*, which is Jesus Christ." That is, I have taught to you Christ as he is, and it is not for any other man to teach anything different.  He declares that " according to the grace of God *which is given unto me*, as a wise master-builder, I have laid the foundation." . . . . . " let every man *take heed how he buildeth thereon*."  Here is a plain intimation that the Christ of Paul rested upon a different foundation from that of Apollos—the one divine, the other human. " I have planted, Apollos watered."  That is, I have planted the seed that will produce the true fruit, and it is for others only to cultivate and nourish what I have planted.

He tells the Corinthians that they were born unto a knowledge of Christ through his gospel

—that is, through his preaching; and that if they had ten thousand instructors, of these there would not be many who, as spiritual fathers, could reveal to them the truth as he had. "Wherefore, I beseech you, be ye followers of me. For this cause have I sent unto you Timotheus, who is my beloved son, and faithful in the Lord, who shall bring you into remembrance of *my ways which be in Christ, as I teach everywhere in every church.*" (1 *Cor.* iv. 16, 17.) What more conclusive evidence could be asked that Apollos was preaching doctrines different from those of Paul as to the nature of Christ, than that the latter sent Timothy to counteract them? and what other doctrines was the former teaching than those of the Alexandrian school? When Paul says all Asia had turned against him, it could only be on the questions which had sprung up between himself and Apollos. It could not be on account of circumcision, because on this point the Greeks would agree with Paul. It was not on account of different views on the subject of the resurrection, because that was retained and became the foundation of the Christian faith. There was but a single point upon which those who professed Christianity at that day could turn upon Paul, and that is his " ways which be in Christ " as he taught them in all the churches. The quarrels of Paul with the Jews on the subject of circumcision died away in the church not long after his death, drowned out by the Greek and Therapeutæ element ; but the cause of the strife between the followers of Paul and Apollos has continued down, in some form, even to our own times.

It could not be long after his letter to the Corinthians that the doctrines preached by Apollos spread through all the churches of Asia Minor and became the established orthodox faith. Paul, in the Second Epistle to Timothy, says : " All Asia has turned against me." A mere change of name—Therapeutæ to Christian —and the revolution was complete. It was made so rapidly that the world scarce noticed it. The Therapeutæ, who were spread over Europe, Asia, and portions of Africa, disappeared so suddenly that it has always been a problem in history what became of them. But we can find here and there, in the history of the times, evidences that the few friends of Paul did not give up the contest with their powerful foe without a struggle. These struggles come to the surface of history like the bubbles from the mouth of a drowning man.

But little change in doctrines was required to justify the Therapeutæ in taking upon themselves the name of Christians. Christ, with Paul, was a Mediator, and so was the Logos of Philo. "What intelligent person," says the latter, " who views mankind engaged in unworthy and wicked pursuits, but must be grieved to the heart, and call upon that Saviour God, that these crimes may be exterminated, and that by a ransom and price of redemption being given for his soul, it may again obtain its freedom. It pleased God, therefore, to appoint his Logos to be a Mediator. To his Word, the chief and most ancient of all in heaven, the great Author of the world gave this especial gift: that he should stand as a medium (or intercessor) between the Creator and the created; and he is accordingly the Advocate of all mortals." (*Jacob Bryant, quoted in Clarke's Commentaries on St. John's Gospel.*) As the Therapeutæ of

Philo were the descendants of a Jewish colony who had settled in Egypt, and still retained in some degree their Mosaic ideas and belief in the Old Testament, under the light of the school of Alexandria, where the doctrines of Philo were taught, they readily adopted the Alexandrian ideas of the Logos. The belief in some intermediate or mediatorial power between God and man was common to the Jews as well as most other people. Adam, by his disobedience, had broken the law, and if he or his descendants are ever to be restored to the favor of the Creator, it is to be done through the office of a Mediator. The notions of Philo on the nature of the Logos suited the Therapeutæ much better than did those of Paul, and after a short struggle we will discover the Alexandrian dogmas to be the creed of the orthodox. Christ's appearance on earth, his death and resurrection, are what Paul preached, and what the Therapeutæ, who were converted by him, believed. These features were retained in the church after the Philo ideas of the Logos had displaced the Christ of Paul. It was only Paul's doctrine of the descent of Jesus from Mary and Joseph after the flesh that was thrown aside by them. The intervention of the Virgin, at a later period in the history of the church, was the means by which the Christ of Paul was made the Son of God in the sense of the Alexandrian school.

The transition of the Therapeutæ to Christianity was easy. Little or no change was made in the form of the services in the church. According to Eusebius, they sang hymns. They read sacred books and made comments on them as well after as before the change. Like the first Christian community, they held all their property in common. They said grace at table both before and after meals, according to Josephus, which they continued to do after they took the name of Christians. They made no change in their fasts and festivals, and retained the monasteries. The transfer of the form of the Therapeutæ church government to the new church was the work of time, and was not fully effected until the second century. The influence of Paul's name, with other causes, was too strong during the first to permit the change.

A Bishop in a Christian church is the work of the second century. Like every other new feature in its history, we find the first Bishop at Alexandria. Gibbon says: "The extensive commerce of Alexandria, and its proximity to Palestine, gave an easy entrance to the new religion. It was at first embraced by great numbers of the Therapeutæ, or Essenians of the lake Mareotis, a Jewish sect which had abated much of its reverence for the Mosaic ceremonies. The austere life of the Essenians, their fasts and excommunications, the community of goods, the love of celibacy, their zeal for martyrdom, and the warmth though not the purity of their faith, already offered a very lively image of the primitive discipline. It was in the school of Alexandria that the Christian theology appears to have assumed a regular and scientifical form; and when Hadrian visited Egypt he found a church, composed of Jews and of Greeks, sufficiently important to attract the notice of that inquisitive prince." (Ch. xv. (162) (163), vol. I. p. 283.)*

---

* After the author had written out his views as above, he met with the following passages from the writings of Michaelis, the great German critic, quoted in Taylor's *Diegesis*. Of the Therapeutæ, he says they are a "Jewish sect, which began to spread

It is safe to say that it was the Therapeutæ who caused the troubles in the churches in Paul's time and afterwards, because no other sect or society was so extended, and had the power to make the disturbance so universal. Paul could complain of no other, and it was this sect that turned all Asia against him. There is no way to account for the sudden and wonderful increase of Christians in a few years before Paul's death, without we can refer the cause to the sudden conversion of the Therapeutæ to the new religion. When they are suddenly lost to

---

itself at Ephesus, and to threaten great mischief to Christianity in the time (or indeed previous to the time) of St. Paul, on which account, in his epistles to the Ephesians, to the Colossians, and to Timothy, he declares himself openly against them." (*Diegesis*, 58.) Again: "It is evident from the above-mentioned epistles of Paul, that, to the great mortification of the apostle, they insinuated themselves very early into the church." (60.) The writer does not wish to be understood that the disturbances created in the church were confined to Corinth, and that Apollos was the only one who taught during the life of Paul the doctrines of the Alexandrian school. Wherever Paul had founded a church, there the Therapeutæ element was at work. Apollos, by his superior eloquence and learning, was distinguished from a host of agitators, and called forth the special notice of Paul.

sight, the small churches of Paul have grown great in numbers, and spread over Europe and Asia in an incredibly short space of time.

Before going to press, the writer came into the possession of the works of Michaelis, where we find the following passage : "But even before Apollos had received the instructions of Aquila and Priscilla, he taught publicly in the synagogue at Ephesus concerning the Messiah. Hence it is not improbable that the Essenes introduced themselves into the church at Ephesus by means of Apollos, who came from Alexandria, in the neighborhood of which city, according to Philo, the Essenes were not only numerous but were held in high estimation." (Vol. iv. p. 85.) It would seem from this that Apollos only continued to do at Corinth what he first began at Ephesus.

No man of any age suffered so much abuse, nor was there ever one whose memory labored under such a weight of obloquy, as that of Paul during the latter part of the first, and nearly the whole of the second century, and that, too, from those who had been converts to the doctrines taught in the school of Apollos. The first half of the Acts was written, as will be shown, expressly to exalt Peter over him and degrade him from the rank of an Apostle. The Revelation ascribed to St. John is nothing but a bitter tirade of denunciation against Paul and his followers. He is called a liar, "the false prophet," who with the beast was cast alive into a lake of burning fire. He is the great red dragon who stood before the woman ready to devour the child Jesus as soon as he was born, and who warred with Michael and the angels. Paul is not only denounced, but Christ himself is made to declare his status in the Godhead. "I Jesus have sent mine angel to testify unto you these things in the churches." (xxii. 16.) What the things were to which the angel was to bear testimony, sufficiently appears in every portion of the book of Revelation. Why was Paul the subject of so much abuse? There can be but one answer. It was because of the way in which he taught Christ in all the churches, which he had learned from the Apostles in his interviews with them at Jerusalem, and probably from Joseph and Mary themselves, for they occurred about the year A.D. 40.

# CHAPTER V.

Review of the past.—What follows in the future.

LET us assume a stand at the beginning of
Adrian's reign, A.D. 117, and make a survey of
the Christian world as it presents itself at that
day.   A half-century has passed since the death
of Paul.   Since then, Rome has been without a
Christian population.   Driven from the city
through the cruel butcheries of the tyrant, they
took refuge in the provinces, especially Asia
Minor, where they remained until the reign of
Adrian and his successor, the tolerant Antoninus Pius.   In the mean time, the Therapeutan
element of Christianity had been steadily on the
increase, while that of Paul had correspondingly
declined.   The proclamation of Adrian, or rather
his letter to Fundanus, a governor of one of the
provinces, prohibiting the punishment of Christians on account of their religion, was the first
intimation from the capital of the empire that

they could return in safety. From this time Christians began to return to Rome in a steady stream, so that within the next twenty years they had so increased in numbers that they once more take a place in history, and are found mixed up in the history of the imperial city.

But at this time Christians, in their contest with the Pagans, found the evidence of Christianity, as it then stood, not sufficient to contend with the infidelity of the age. The old religion of Rome was hallowed by time, supported by the learned men of that day, and upheld by the power of the State. The Gospels had not yet appeared; the world was without a miracle; Mary, the bride of Heaven, afterwards the central figure in the Hierarchy of the orthodox, had no place in history. Peter had not been in Rome, or John in Asia. The personal influence of Paul and his immediate followers had kept alive the spirit of Christianity in Asia; but now Paul is no more, and the influence of his name has nearly passed away. The proof that there ever were such persons as Christ and his disciples had become faint. The dim light of tradition, and what Paul, and his companion Bar-

3*

nabas, said of him in their epistles, comprised
about all the evidence at that day to sustain the
claims of Christianity.  But Paul himself had
not seen Christ, except under such circumstances as might excite suspicion of either delusion
or fraud.  He had seen Peter, and remained
with him, in the first place fifteen days; and
afterwards went to Jerusalem, where he saw all of
the disciples who were then living.  What Paul
learned from the disciples, with his vision near
Damascus, was sufficient to convince him of the
reality of Christ and the truth of the religion he
taught.  But the proof all lay within himself.
The genuine epistles of Peter, as we will show,
were so corrupted by the men of the second
century, that we have no means of knowing how
much of the original remains or how much has
been added.  The epistle of James, which is the
only writing by an Apostle, or any one else,
that has come down to us from the Apostolic
age without some evidence of fraud and corruption, only speaks of Christ as a just man, and
makes no mention of the prodigies and wonders
claimed to have taken place at the time of his
birth and death; nor does he take notice of the

miracles and wonderful things spoken of in the Gospels. The proof, whatever it may have been, that Christ ever existed, was too weak to overcome or even contend against the skepticism of the age.

So far we have said nothing of the Hebrew Gospel of Matthew, because it was cast to one side, for the reason that it was a standing argument against the Alexandrian ideas of the Logos—and was regarded as of no authority in the church until it had been improved by important additions made afterwards, and passed into the present Greek version. With such proof as existed at the time we write of, Christianity could not hold its ground against the great pressure brought to bear it down—much less make headway against such powerful opposition. The time to supply new proof of the reality of Christ was favorable. All the scenes in his life lay within the boundaries of Galilee, Samaria, and Judea—the greater part in and about Jerusalem. Since his death the Legions of Rome had been there, and left nothing standing except a few towers, reserved for military defence. The silence of death, for almost a half century,

had reigned in the streets of Jerusalem. · The
greater part of the Jewish people had been put
to death by the sword, or carried away into
captivity.   All who lived during the time of
Christ, by age and the calamities of war had
gone to their graves.   We shall soon see the
Synoptics appear in intervals such as circumstances demanded, each bearing the name of
an Apostle, or the name of some one who wrote
at their dictation.   A little further down in the
century we will find men engaged in laying the
foundation of a church, whose claims to infalli-
bility and supremacy are based on " apostolic
succession."   When we come to this period we
will find all ecclesiastical history to consist of
traditions, and a time in the world's life which
is populated by Bishops and high-church dig-
nitaries, who pass before us without speech or
action, like shadows on a wall.   We shall find
Peter has been in Rome ; John at Ephesus ;
Paul in Gaul, Spain, and Britain.   We will find
parties engaged in exalting Peter above all the
other Apostles—and the same influence at work
to put down Paul.   Again we will see Paul restored to favor, but his writings defaced by for-

gcrics, to conform to the doctrines of the day. We shall also see Christians enter into quarrels among themselves, which continue through centuries. Books are forged, traditions manufactured, and the works of the Fathers shamefully altered and corrupted. Later in the century, brought out by a pressure which made it necessary, the fourth Gospel will appear, and Christianity pass from the Alexandrian Logos to the Incarnate God. By casting our eyes still further down the centuries, we will see Christianity and the philosophy of Plato strangely allied, which brings us to the era of the Trinity. Let us first inquire into the origin of the three first Gospels.

# CHAPTER VI.

### HOW THE FOUR GOSPELS ORIGINATED.

THE origin of the Gospels has proved a Serbonian bog, in which many writers who have attempted an explanation have floundered without finding solid ground. Scarce two writers agree. Why should there be any doubt in a matter of so much importance, where the evidence could so readily be obtained at the time they were written, and so safely guarded and preserved? Truth, in a historic period like that in which it is claimed the Gospels were written, need not be left in the dark. The true difficulty has grown out of the fact, that writers who have undertaken to give the origin of the Gospels have looked, as men do in most other cases, to outside sources for information ; whereas the explanation of the origin is to be found within the Gospels themselves, and nowhere else. By looking for light where none is to be found, writers on this subject have had their attention withdrawn from the direction where the truth is to be discovered. If we bear in mind that men eighteen hundred years ago were much like men of to-day, that the emotion or effect a given event or occurrence produces in the minds of men of our own time would be the same as upon those who lived in the first part of the second century, we have a compass, such as it is, to guide us through this Cimmerian darkness. What would excite ridicule, or appear false and improbable to intelligent minds of our own times, would appear equally so to such minds as Pliny and Tacitus at their ages of the world.

In imagination let us take a stand at the beginning of the second century, and make ourselves citizens of the Roman empire under the reign of Adrian. We can well imagine how the minds of thinking and intelligent people were affected on the first appearance of the present Greek version of Matthew's Gospel. It set forth some of the most astounding events in the history of the world, and which the world heard of for the *first time*. When Christ was put to death, all the land, from the sixth to the ninth hour, was covered with darkness; the veil of the temple was rent in twain from the top to the bottom; the earth did quake, and the rocks were rent asunder; the graves were opened, and many bodies of saints which slept arose and came out of their graves, and went into the holy city and appeared unto many. Suppose that some morning we should pick up our daily paper, and find under the telegraph head an announcement of like events as having occurred in London or Paris. At first we might be fearfully startled, but would soon feel satisfied that it was all a hoax, after the style of Professor Locke's story of the Moon. If the authors of the story expected to accomplish anything by such startling announcements, they failed by attempting too much. Whether the earth was covered with darkness, or was shaken by an earthquake, or the dead got out of their graves and went down into the city, were facts easily inquired into, in that age of the world.

Matthew further states that a star went before the wise men of the East, till it came and stood over where the young child was. How could a star a million of miles off lead any one on this earth, and how could it at that distance be in a position to indicate a spot on the earth where the child was ?   He also states, that when Herod found he was mocked he was wroth, and sent forth and slew all the children that were in *Bethlehem* and all the coast thereof, from two years old and under.   We can readily imagine the Pagans, who composed the learned and intelligent men of their day, at work in exposing the story of Herod's cruelty, by showing that, considering the extent of territory embraced in the order, and the population within it, the assumed destruction of life stamped the story false and ridiculous.   A Governor of a Roman province who dared make such an order would be so speedily overtaken by the vengeance of the Roman people, that his head would fall from his body before the blood of his victims had time to dry.   Archelaus, his son, was deposed for offences not to be spoken of when compared with this massacre of the infants.

But that part of the first Gospel which re-related to the dream of Joseph and the conception of Mary was what most excited the criticism and ridicule of the people of that day. The whole and sole foundation of the new religion was *a dream*. The simplicity of Joseph, too, provoked a smile, if nothing more. The story at the sepulchre was overdrawn, and threw discredit over all. " And behold, there was a great earthquake : for the angel of the Lord descended from heaven, and came and rolled back the stone from the door, and sat upon it. His countenance was like lightning, and his raiment white as snow." (*Matthew* xxviii. 2, 3.) Such aërial bodies are not given to the employments assigned to the angel in this case. Rolling stones, say the wise men, by spiritual essences is ridiculous and absurd. Besides, who knows anything of the great earthquake ? We find no account of it, nor is it even mentioner anywhere else.

So men reasoned eighteen hundred years ago —and so they would to-day. It is evident that the author of the first Gospel had overdone his part, and injured the cause he meant to advance. The blunders and mistakes of the first Gospel made it necessary that there should be a second. This gave rise to a second Gospel, not by the same hand, but by some other, who felt the pressure that had been brought to bear on Matthew.

As this second Gospel was written with a special purpose, we must expect a great resemblance in it to the first, except where the former makes statements which were the occasion of so much criticism on the part of the philosophers; and in such cases, the best course to pursue would be to say nothing. Naked contradiction would not answer. Mark has not a word to say about the story of Joseph and the angel. He omits the earthquake at the crucifixion, and the resurrection of the dead, for these things were susceptible of disproof; but tells of the darkness, and the rent in the temple, because the former was comparative, and may have been a dark cloud in the heavens; and as to the case of the temple, no one could disprove the story, for it was destroyed. The story of the angel and stone is entirely omitted, but the stone is removed from the mouth of the sepulchre when the women appear, and a young man is found in the inside, who is presumed to have done it. Matthew says that Joseph of Arimathea deposited the body of Christ in the sepulchre, and then rolled a great stone to the door. Afterwards the priest and Pharisees caused the entrance to be made *secure*, for fear that the body would be stolen, and the disciples then claim that he had risen from the dead. If so, say the philosophers, the work was not so poorly done that *one* young man could roll the stone from the door, as stated by Mark. It would be beyond his strength.

Luke removes the objection; when the women come to the sepulchre in the morning they found the stone removed, and the body of Christ was missing. There was no young man inside, but *two* men were found standing on the outside, who, no doubt, were competent to do the work. The story of the star which lĕd the wise men, and the murder of the infants at Bethlehem, is also omitted. We are justified in saying that those who were engaged in getting up the *first* Gospel, or those who succeeded them, were driven to abandon some false and impossible and improbable things stated in that Gospel, by proof, in some cases, of their falsehood, and in others by the force of argument and ridicule.

Matthew had related the story of Joseph and the angel, and that admitted of no change or modification. Mark says nothing about it, but silence will not answer; for the philosophers still claim that all depends upon a *dream*, and the dreams of Joseph are no better than the dreams of any other man. If the story could not be modified, it might be corroborated. So, when it came to Luke's turn to speak he adds the story of Zacharias, and the interview between Mary and the angel Gabriel. All now occurs in *daylight*, and dreams which had been the subject of so much ridicule are dispensed with.

When Zacharias went to the temple to burn incense, he found on the outside a great multitude of people. The crowd has no connection with the story, except as these people are wanted for witness as to what happened *in the sanctuary*. While Zacharias was offering incense within, there appeared to him an angel standing on the right side of the altar. The position of the angel is defined with precision, that it might not be claimed that what appeared to him was a phantom. Zacharias saw him and was afraid.

As further evidence that the angel was not some optical illusion, Gabriel spoke, and gave Zacharias such information about the future birth of a son to him that he was disposed to doubt the truth of it. As a punishment for his reasonable doubts, he is struck dumb. The interview continued so long that the crowd on the outside began to be uneasy, and when Zacharias did come out he had lost the power of speech. This convinced the multitude (but how, is not stated) that he had seen a vision in the temple. After this, Gabriel made a visit to Mary in open day, and held a conversation, in which he announced to her the birth of a son through the overshadowing influence of the Holy Ghost, who would reign over the house of Jacob forever. Then follows the scene between Mary and her cousin Elisabeth.

In Luke's account of the announcement of the birth of Christ by divine agency, the story of Joseph is entirely omitted, and new witnesses are introduced. His story was well studied; every precaution was taken to silence cavil and make such a case as would remove doubts. The blunders of Matthew were not to be repeated. The birth of Christ and John, who was afterwards called the Baptist, are ingeniously associated in the announcement of the angel, to give color to what is said of them in the Gospels afterwards.

What objections were made by the philosophers to the story of Luke at the time, we have no means of knowing; but if any were made, there is no subsequent effort to improve it, and so it remains to this day.

The question interests us to know when and from whom did Luke get his information. If he had it from any one who had the means of knowing what he tells us, it must have been from Paul, for we have no knowledge that he had any acquaintance, or relations of any kind, with either of the disciples. He was Paul's companion: we find him with Paul at Troas, A.D. 50; thence he attended him to Jerusalem, continued with him during his troubles in Judea, and sailed in the same ship with him when he was sent a prisoner to Rome, where he stayed with him during his two years' confinement. He was with him during his second imprisonment, and, as we will show in the proper place, he died with Paul in Rome, and was one of the victims of Nero's reign. If Paul knew what Luke states as to the divine emanation of Christ, why does he not make some allusion to it in his numerous epistles ?—and how can we understand that he could, with such knowledge, deny this divine creation, and preach to the last that Christ was born according to natural law ?

Luke, too, made mistakes, which John afterwards corrected in the fourth Gospel.

We can best illustrate the claim that the three last Gospels were written in the order they appeared, as a necessity to meet the objections and cavils of the philosophers, by taking some leading subject which is mentioned by all. Take the case of the *resurrection*. Matthew says : " And when they saw him, they worshipped him : but some doubted." (Matt. xxviii. 17.) To leave the question where Matthew leaves it would be fatal. In such a case there must be no doubt. Mark makes Christ appear three times under such circumstances as to render a mistake next to impossible, and to silence the most obstinate skepticism. He first appears to Mary Magdalene, who was convinced that it was Christ, because she went and told the disciples that he had risen, and that she had seen him. They disbelieved, nor could they be convinced until he appeared to them. They in turn told it to the other disciples, who were also skeptical; and, that they might be convinced, Christ also appeared to them as they sat at meat, when he upbraided them for their unbelief.

This story is much improved in the hands of Mark, but, in the anxiety to make a clear case, it is overdone, as often happens when the object is to remedy or correct an oversight or mistake previously made. There was a large amount of skepticism to be overcome, but the proof offered was sufficient to do it, and remove all doubts from the minds of the disciples. Considering Christ had told the disciples he would rise, why did they doubt at all? Owing to some strange oversight, neither Matthew nor Mark says in what way Christ made his appearance—whether it was in the body or only in the spirit. If in the latter, it would be fatal to the whole theory of the resurrection. We conclude from what followed, that the philosophers of that day, who would concede nothing to the claims of Christi-

4

anity, took advantage of this oversight, and denied the resurrection of Christ in the body. It was the business of Luke to put this disputed question in its true light, and silence the objection. He says that when Christ appeared and spoke to the disciples they were afraid. " But they were terrified and affrighted, and supposed that they had seen a *spirit.*" (*Luke* xxiv. 37.) Christ then showed the wounds in his hands and feet. " And they gave him a piece of a *broiled* fish, and of a *honeycomb*. And he took it, and did *eat before them.*" (*Luke* xxiv. 42, 43.) Now who dare doubt? Why some doubted, as Matthew says they did, is hard to explain. The account of Luke should have satisfied the philosophers that it was a body and not a spirit that appeared to the disciples. But we can believe they were not, from what is afterwards said on this subject. The story of the fish and honeycomb was incredible and absurd. It was a fish-story. If true, why did Matthew and Mark fail to mention it ?

Luke had overdone the matter, and instead of convincing the Pagans, he only excited their ridicule.

Now comes John's turn. He does not omit entirely the story of Christ eating fish, for that would not do, after there had been so much said about it. He might leave it to be inferred that Luke made a mistake, so he modifies the story and omits the ridiculous part of it. The scene is laid on the shores of the Sea of Tiberias. Under the direction of Christ, Peter drew his net to land full of fish. " Jesus saith unto them, Come and dine. And none of the disciples durst ask him, Who art thou ? knowing that it was the Lord. Jesus then cometh, and taketh *bread, and giveth them, and fish* likewise." (*John* xxi. 12, 13.) It does not appear from this account that Christ ate of the fish at all. He took the fish and gave to the disciples ; the inference is, that they were the ones that ate. In Luke the statement is reversed ;—the disciples gave the fish to Christ, and he ate. John has taken out of the story that which was absurd, but he leaves us to infer that Luke was *near-sighted* or *careless* in his account of what took place. If you leave out of Luke's account the part that relates to the fish and honeycomb, he fails to prove what it really was which appeared to the disciples.

Christ, he says, said, " Behold my hands and my feet, that it is I myself." (Ch. xxiv. 39.) " And while they yet believed not for joy, and wondered, he said unto them, Have ye here any meat ? " (Ch. xxiv. 41.) It seems from this that the disciples could not be convinced until Christ had actually eaten something. Now if you strike out the eating part, which John does, and which no doubt the ridicule cast upon it drove him to do, Luke leaves the question open just where he found it. It was the business of John to leave it clean, and put an end to all cavil.

Jesus appeared to the disciples when they assembled at Jerusalem. " And when he had so said, he shewed unto them his hands and his side." (*John* xx. 20.) They were satisfied, and no doubts were expressed. But Thomas was not present, and when he was told that Jesus had appeared to the disciples, he refused to believe, nor would he, " Except I shall see in his hands the print of the nails, and put my finger into the print of the nails, and thrust my hand into his side, I will not believe." (*John* xx. 25.) Now if Thomas can be convinced with all his doubts, it would be foolish after that to deny that Christ was not in the body when he appeared to his disciples.

After eight days Christ again appears, without any object that we can discover but to convince Thomas. Then said he to Thomas, "Reach hither thy finger, and behold my hands; and reach hither thy hand, and thrust it into my side; and be not faithless, but believing." (*John* xx. 27.) It is not stated whether he did as he was directed; but he was convinced, and exclaimed, "*My Lord and my God.*"

What fault the Pagans found with this account we have not the means of knowing; but if they still disbelieved, they were more skeptical than Thomas himself. We should be at a loss to understand why the writers of the three first Gospels entirely omitted the story of Thomas, if we were not aware that when John wrote the state of the public mind was such, that proof of the most unquestionable character was demanded that Christ had risen in the body. John selected a person who claimed he was hard to convince, and if the evidence was such as to satisfy him, it ought to satisfy the balance of the world.

John's services are again required to repair the blunders and oversights of the writers of the three first Gospels in relation to the body of Christ after the crucifixion. Matthew states that Mary Magdalene and the other Mary went on the first day of the week to see the sepulchre. No other purpose is expressed. Mark says that early in the morning of the first day of the week, Mary Magdalene and Mary the mother of James and Salome brought spices to anoint the body. According to Luke, after the women who had followed Christ from Galilee had seen the body deposited in the tomb, they returned and prepared spices and ointments, and rested the Sabbath day. The body was deposited in the tomb some time on Friday, and remained until Sunday morning, on the first day of the Jewish week. Doubtless, in the climate of Syria, the body in the mean time must have undergone such a change as to make it difficult to either embalm or even anoint it. The Pagans at that day could hardly fail to take advantage of this mistake or blunder. But John again comes to the rescue and sets the matter right. According to him, Joseph of Arimathea had permission to take the body, which he did, and carried it away. "And there came also Nicodemus (which at the first came to Jesus by night) and brought a mixture of myrrh and aloes, *about a hundred pounds weight.* Then took they the body of Jesus, and wound it in linen clothes with the spices, as the manner of the Jews is to bury." (*John* xix. 39, 40.)

John now fully silenced the cavils of the enemy and taken the proper steps to preserve the body until the morning of the third day.

The subject might be further pursued, but enough has been said to furnish a key to the origin of the Gospels. Christians in their contests with the Pagans resemble the course of a retreating army, which falls back to take a stronger position. Each time the position is improved, until one at last is found which is impregnable. We can readily see how it is that the three first Gospels so closely resemble each other, the exact language for whole passages being alike in all. Mark copies Matthew, and Luke uses the words of both. It is only

when the last undertakes to improve or modify
something, written by those who wrote previously, that the difference becomes obvious.
That the Christians in the beginning of the second century had books of some kind before
the three first Gospels appeared in the present
shape, is beyond all dispute. The sacred writings of the Therapeutæ, as we have shown,
were full of the most sound morality, and contained all the essential principles of Christianity.
These writings were ancient—had been regarded
as sacred for generations among them, and were
so much like the present Gospels that Eusebius
claimed them to be the same, and that the
Therapeutæ were Christians. No doubt the
Hebrew Gospel of Matthew was extant, and if
it was rejected by the Christians of that day,
because it did not contain the two first chapters
of the Greek version, there was no reason why
they should reject the Sermon on the Mount,
and all the sublime and pure religion taught by
Christ. The sacred writings of the Therapeutæ
—the Hebrew version of Matthew, the Epistle
of James and the first of Peter furnished the principles and doctrines which now form the life of

Christianity, and the great want of the day—that is, some proof of the actual existence of the person of Christ, by those who had seen him and were familiar with him before his death—was supplied in the three first Gospels, by the testimony of those who claimed to be his disciples, or by those who, it is said, wrote at their dictation.

In what quarter of the globe were the Synoptics written, and by whom? All that can be said on this subject with certainty is, that the Greek version of Matthew, the source of all, was not written in Judea, or by one who knew anything of the geography of the country, or the history of the Jews. He was ignorant of both. What excuse was there but ignorance for making the order for the massacre of the infants to include Bethlehem, and all *the coast thereof*, which would take in at least the one-half of all Judea, and involve in one common slaughter, according to the calculations of learned men, several thousand innocent children? The Greek writer of Matthew evidently believed that Bethlehem was an insignificant hamlet, situated on the coast of the Mediterranean, whereas it is as far in the interior as Jerusalem, and not far from the centre of Judea. The writer's ignorance of Jewish history will appear still more conspicuous, when we speak of the application which he makes of prophecy to the person of Jesus. Whoever the writer may have been, it is evident that he received his education at the college at Alexandria, where Medicine and Divinity were taught, and regarded as inseparable. From the union of the two, recovery from diseases was ascribed to supernatural powers. A fever was a demon, which was not to be expelled by virtue of any material remedy, but by incantations, spells, and magic. It was by such power Christ cleansed the leper—healed the centurion's servant—touched the hand of Peter's wife's mother and drove away the fever —expelled the devils from two men into swine, and performed many other cures. The whole of the first Gospel has an Alexandrian look not easily to be mistaken—if we except the miracle of the loaves and fishes—walk of Christ on the water, and other wonders of a like nature, which is the work of some one later in the century. The deserts in the neighborhood of

Alexandria abounded with monasteries from the earliest accounts of the Therapeutæ to the conquest of Egypt by the Mahometan power, which were filled with monks who were celebrated for their piety, their miracles, their power to expel devils and heal diseases. The pages of Sozomen and Socrates abound with the names of monks who cured the palsy, expelled demons, and cured the sick. (Sozomen, *Ecc. Hist.*, lib. vi., ch. 28.)

# CHAPTER VII.

John the son of Zebedee never in Asia Minor.—John the Presbyter substituted.—The work of Irenæus and Eusebius.—John the disciple has served to create an enigma in history.—John of Ephesus a myth.

WAS John the son of Zebedee ever in Asia ? To ask a question which implies a doubt on a subject on which the world has been agreed for almost two centuries, will probably startle many even in this age of inquiry and progress. It may be a question, whether he who makes a discovery in science or the arts which facilitates the advance of mankind, or he who contributes by his labors to remove a delusion which has stood in the way of progress, is most entitled to the gratitude of his fellow-men. A falsehood, as long as it stands unquestioned, may and does receive the respect which is due to the truth ; but there is a time when, no matter how hoary with age, it must pass away and give place to the latter.

John the son of Zebedee the fisherman, upon careful inquiry, can never be successfully confounded with him of Ephesus. His character, as developed in the Synoptics, is composed of negative qualities. We find him in Jerusalem when he had got to be fifty years old, without any evidence, up to that time, that he had been out of sight of the walls of the city, and no proof that he said or did anything worthy of notice. His name is mentioned in connection with some of the great scenes in the life of Christ, but he takes no part, and, like the supernumeraries on the stage, his presence is only needed to fill up a required number. To be sure, Paul speaks of him in connection with James and Peter as pillars of the church—which has no significance, as the nine other disciples were all moderate men, and the church at the time few in number and easily managed. John of the Synoptics is not only lymphatic and of negative qualities, but, from his condition in life and pursuits, must have had but little learning of any kind. John of the Greeks is a man of learning, and a scholar. He was master of the Greek, and was familiar with the abstruse and subtle philosophy of that specula-

tive people.   He was at home in all the different
and various doctrines of the Gnostics, and proved
himself the most able man of the age in his contests with those numerous sects which embraced
the most learned men of the second century.
In fine, this John of Galilee, whose name is seldom mentioned, or if so, not for anything he
said or did, who lives to be more than fifty without the least notice being taken of him, or allusion made—this phlegmatic John, after he has
passed the meridian of life, and his powers are
on the decline, has all at once become a teacher,
and the great light of Grecian theology, and
wields a pen with the fire and spirit of Demos-
thenes !   A change and complete transformation
like this is nowhere else to be found in the history of the world.   The truth is, the John of
Galilee is not the John of Ephesus.   The latter
is a phantom of some Greek's brain, which has
served to mislead men for ages.

If John the disciple had ever passed out of Syria into Asia Minor, so important a fact would
find a place in some authentic history ; and from
the time he put his foot in the country, his mean-
derings, like those of Paul, would be well known

and preserved. We leave him in Jerusalem in A.D. 50, and the next time we hear of him he is in Ephesus. When he left Judea, and when he arrived in Asia Minor, no one pretends to know. From the year forty-eight, and perhaps much sooner, to the spring of sixty-five, Paul spent nine-tenths of his time travelling up and down the Archipelago, establishing and visiting the churches. He made the circuit three times, and it was his uniform practice, in closing his epistles to the different churches, to mention those of the brethren who were with him, even if they were not of much importance ; and yet in none of them does he mention the name of John. Considering that John was an Apostle, this silence of Paul can be accounted for only by the fact that he did not hear of or see him in Asia Minor, and was in Ephesus as late as the year sixty-four, and still later, sixty-five, and up to that time John had not been there, for Paul makes no mention of him.

What historical proof is there that is worthy of credit, that John was ever in Asia Minor ? The whole story rests on the shoulders of Irenæus. Here is what he says : " Then, again, the church in Ephesus, founded by Paul, and having John remaining among them permanently until the times of Trajan, is a true witness of the traditions." (Book III. sec. 3.) Irenæus cites no authority, and we have a right, in a matter of so much importance, to demand of him some evidence that what he states is true. In this absence of any reference to written testimony we have a right to infer that there was none, and that there was no ground for the assertion but tradition. This Irenæus is forced to admit. The book on heresies was written, as we shall show, about A.D. 181. According to authentic history, Paul was in Ephesus in sixty-five, the last time. If the statement of Irenæus is founded on tradition, and there is no other, then the tradition that Paul left John in Ephesus is one hundred and sixteen years old. We will see what a tradition so old, handed down to future ages, is worth, coming from Irenæus.

A tradition over one hundred years old, when first inserted into the pages of history by one of the most dishonest historians of any age, is the authority we have in our day for believing a most important fact in the history of the Christian church. The caption to the section from which the above passage was taken will explain the reason why Irenæus undertook to misrepresent the truth of history: *"A refutation of the heretics, from the fact that, in the various churches, a perpetual succession of Bishops was kept up."* He was engaged in furnishing an apostle to the churches in Asia Minor and some parts of Greece, for an "apostolic succession." We will find him engaged in doing a great deal of this kind of business before we are done with him. The proof that John was not in Ephesus is conclusive. The language of Irenæus implies that Paul placed John in charge of the church when he left for Rome *for he says John remained.* This is not so. When Paul left Ephesus, in the year A. D. 64 or 65, he left Timothy there in charge of the church, and he remained until Paul got into trouble in Rome, in the fall of A. D. 65, when the latter sent for him. Would Paul leave the church in the charge of Timothy when one of the Apostles was there, especially as he was so young that some objected to him on account of his age? In writing to Timothy to meet him in Rome, would Paul fail to make some mention of the Apostle, if he had been in Ephesus when he left?—Not one word to an Apostle who would naturally take charge of the church, in the absence of himself and Timothy?

It is clear, then, that John had not been in Ephesus up to the fall or summer of A. D. 65, when Timothy left to go to Rome; and the question is, was he there after this? and if so, when? Polycarp presided over the church at Smyrna, which was not far from Ephesus, and between the two points there was constant intercourse by land and water; and if John had succeeded Timothy at the latter place, would not he, Polycarp, take some notice of so important a fact? He speaks of Paul in his letter to the Philippians, and why not mention John, who was one of the twelve Apostles? Polycarp lived to the end of the century, and it is claimed John also lived to about that time, and as they both lived so long in such close proximity, how natural it would be that the intercourse between them should be most intimate, and that the former should mention those relations with an Apostle in writing to the churches he addressed.

Irenæus felt the force of this, and undertakes to show that Polycarp was the *hearer and disciple of John.* He says: "These things are attested by Papias, who was John's hearer and the associate of Polycarp, an ancient writer, who mentions them in the fourth book of his works." (Quoted in Eusebius, *Ecc. Hist.*, book iii., chap. 39.) It is meant that it should be understood from this passage that both Papias and Polycarp had seen and heard John the Apostle. Now Papias never conversed with John, the son of Zebedee the fisherman, and he says so, in a fragment preserved in the writings of Eusebius. After quoting the passage just cited from Irenæus, Eusebius says: "But Papias himself, in the preface to his discourses, by no means asserts that he was a hearer and an eye-witness of the holy Apostles, but informs us that he received the doctrines of faith *from their intimate friends*, which he states in the following words: 'But I shall not regret to subjoin to my interpretations, also for your benefit, whatsoever I have at any time accurately ascertained and treasured up in my memory, as I have received it *from the elders*, and have recorded it in order to give

additional confirmation to the truth by my testimony.   For I never, like many, delighted to
hear those that tell many things, but those that
teach the truth ; neither those that record foreign
precepts, but those that are given from the Lord
to our faith, and that came from the truth itself.
But if I met with any one who had been a fol-
lower of the elders anywhere, I made it a point
to inquire what were the declarations of the
elders,—what was said by Andrew, Peter, or
Philip ; what by Thomas, James, John, Matthew, or any other of the disciples of our Lord ;
what was said by Aristion, and the Presbyter
John, disciples of the Lord ; for I do not think
that I derived so much benefit from books as
from the living voice of those that are still sur-
viving.'   And the same Papias of whom we now
speak professes to have received the declaration
of the Apostles *from those that were in company
with them*, and says also that he was a hearer of
Aristion and the Presbyter John.   For, as he
has often mentioned them by name, he also
gives their statements in his own works."   (Eusebius, *Ecc. Hist.*, book iii. chap. 39.)

He says he never conversed with John, but

with the elders, and that *he was a hearer of Presbyter John, and so was Polycarp.* When Irenæus says that Papias conversed with John, without telling which John, he knew that no one would be thought of but the disciple ; and such would have been the case, had not Eusebius preserved this fragment from the writings of Papias. Polycarp and Papias both conversed with the same John, who was John the Presbyter. In another place Irenæus says : " But Polycarp also was only instructed by this Apostle, and had conversed with many who had seen Christ." (Book iii. chap. 3, sec. 3.) This is a palpable falsehood, and so appears from the passage just cited. He cites no authority, but lets facts of so much importance in history depend on his simple word. If what is stated be true, why does not Polycarp himself say something about the sources from which he derived his doctrines ? Nothing would give so great weight to his preaching as that he derived what he taught from those who had listened to Christ and his Apostles. Why speak of Paul, and what he taught, and not of Jesus and his disciples, and what they taught ?

The world is indebted to Irenæus for the story of what took place between John and Cerinthus at the bath-house in Ephesus. Speaking of Polycarp, and how in all respects he was superior to Valentinianus and Marcion, he says: "*There are also those* who heard from him (Polycarp) that John, the disciple of the Lord, going to bathe at Ephesus, and perceiving Cerinthus within, rushed out of the bath-house without bathing, exclaiming, 'Let us fly, lest even the bath-house fall down, because Cerinthus is within.'" (Book iii. chap. 3.)

Now it has been shown that John the disciple of the Lord never saw Polycarp, and if anything of the kind ever did take place, it was between Polycarp and John the Presbyter. The latter is a historic character, spoken of by Polycarp, who lived about this time, and was a Presbyter in the church; and it is evident that Irenæus seeks to confound the Apostle with him. It is for this reason he describes him in the above passage as "the disciple of the Lord," for which there was no reason, unless he meant to deceive. We have proved that he tried it once, and when the first falsehood is uttered it is easy to fabricate a second. This is the first blow that was directed by Irenæus against Cerinthus, a leader among the Gnostics ; but it is only initiatory to still heavier ones which are to follow.

Marcion was a distinguished character among the Gnostics, and he too must receive some damaging blows at the hands of Polycarp, the disciple of John. And Polycarp himself replied to Marcion, who met him on one occasion, and said, " Dost thou know me ?"—" I do know thee—the first-born of Satan."—" Such," continues the writer, " was the horror which the *Apostles and the disciples* had against holding even a verbal communication with any of the corrupters of the truth." (Book iii. chap. 3.)

The Apostle in this case was John the Presbyter, if any one, and the disciple Polycarp the martyr, who had, in fact, never seen any of the Apostles. It is to be noted that no authority is given by Irenæus for these stories, though they are introduced as some things which somebody had said. Such is history.

The value of tradition from the authority of Irenæus may be judged of by the following statement he makes, evidently intended to strengthen the assertion he made about the presence of St. John in Asia Minor. In all cases where he wants it to appear that the Apostle was there, he connects the principal subject with other statements in a way as if the main fact was incidentally mentioned. "Now Jesus was, as it were, beginning to be thirty years old when he came to receive baptism, and according to those men he preached only one year, reckoning from his baptism. On completing his thirtieth year he suffered, being still a young man, and who had by no means attained to advanced age. Now, that the first stage of early life embraces thirty years, and that extends onwards to the fortieth year, every one will admit ; but from the fortieth and fiftieth year a man begins to decline towards old age, which our Lord possessed, while he still fulfilled the office of teacher, even as the gospel and all the elders testify." "Those who were conversant in Asia with John, the disciple of the Lord (affirming) that John gave to them that information. And he remained among them up to the time of Trajan. Some of them, moreover, saw not only John, but the other Apostles, and heard the same account from them, and bear testimony as to the validity of the statement. Which, then, should we rather believe? — whether such as these, or Ptolemæus, who never saw the Apostles, and who never in his dreams attained to the slightest trace of an Apostle?" (Book ii. chap. 22, sec. 5.)

It seems that Irenæus had got into a dispute with Ptolemæus, and attempts to silence him, as he does all opponents, by the authority of the disciples, and especially of John, who is the only one he names. John, too, was in Asia at the time. It is not said where the other Apostles were. Ptolemæus claimed, as appears in the first part of the same section, "that Christ preached for one year only, and then suffered in the twelfth month." The argument with Ptolemæus was, that Christ was too young, and preached too short a time, to be regarded as a teacher of much authority; and in this way, as Irenæus says, "destroying his whole work, and robbing him of that age which is both necessary and more honorable than any other; that more advanced age, I mean, during which also, as a teacher, he excelled all others." The objection is put down in a summary way, claiming that the time of Christ's preaching extended over a period of *ten years.* This is what the Apostles stated, *and what John said while he was in Asia, and who remained there to the time of the death of Trajan.*

Now, the proof taken from evangelical history, and all other sources, shows that the ministry of Christ extended over little more than three years. Did John, while he was in Asia, and the other Apostles, no matter where, give rise to such absurd and false traditions? If John was in Ephesus at the time Paul went to Rome, in the year A. D. 65, and remained to the time of Trajan, as stated by Irenæus, he was in Asia thirty-five years. During this time his history must have been so interwoven with the affairs of the church, holding the rank of an Apostle, that nothing could be more easy than to prove his presence in the country. There is no difficulty in following the footsteps of Paul for each year after he set out to preach the gospel, whether in Europe or Asia; and so with any real character who has been conspicuous for his talents, or from the position he held in his day. But neither Irenæus nor Eusebius have been able to furnish the world with the least evidence of a substantial character of the presence of John in Asia, although they have undertaken it, and exhausted their ingenuity in trying to do so. If no better proof can be given of the presence of John in Asia, after a residence of thirty-five years, than a grave, which may as well be claimed to be that of Hannibal as that of John, the world will be satisfied he never was there. Eusebius has displayed his characteristic ingenuity, and shown his usual disregard for truth in an effort to prove that the grave of John was in Ephesus, and that it was identified as late as the latter part of the second or beginning of the third century. He travels out of his way to do it—manifests from the way he does it that he is engaged in a fraud, and, between the fear of detection and anxiety for success, he makes poor work of it. He causes Polycrates, who was Bishop of Ephesus, to write a letter to Victor, Bishop of Rome, with the apparent purpose of informing him that some mighty luminaries had fallen asleep in Asia, but, in fact, to give an opportunity to make mention of the grave of John as being there in Ephesus. Who these luminaries were who had fallen asleep, he does not name; but dismisses this part of the subject and proceeds to say: " Moreover, John, that rested on the bosom of our Lord, he also rests at Ephesus." Some other matters are introduced into the letter, which related to the burial of Philip and his two daughters at Hierapolis; but this was only intended to conceal the real purpose and design of the writer.

Victor was Bishop of Rome in the beginning of the second century, after John, if we admit he was in Asia, had been dead one hundred years. In writing to Victor about persons who had lately died, and without saying who they were, why should Polycrates make mention of the grave of John as located in Ephesus, which, if true, would have been as well known to all Asia as the tomb of Washington is known to the enlightened world to be at Mount Vernon?

That intelligent men of the second and third centuries denied and disproved the presence of John in Asia, is rendered certain by the struggles and desperate efforts of their adversaries to establish the affirmative. The indications are, that the philosophers proved that the person whom the Christians claimed to be the Apostle John was some other John ; in all probability, John the Presbyter.   Upon this point the proof seems to have been so conclusive that the Christians were driven to the necessity of proving that there were two Johns—one besides the presbyter. Eusebius takes this task upon himself.  We quote from the above letter of Polycrates to Victor : " For in Asia also mighty luminaries have fallen asleep, which will rise again at the last day at the appearance of the Lord, when he shall come with glory from heaven, and shall gather again all the saints.   Philip, one of the twelve Apostles, sleeps in Hierapolis, and his two aged virgin daughters.   Another of his daughters, who lived in the Holy Spirit, rests at Ephesus.   Moreover, John, that rested on the bosom of the Lord, who was a priest that bore the sacerdotal plate, and martyr, and teacher, he also rests at Ephesus."  (Eusebius, *Ecc. Hist.*, book iii. ch. 31.)  Owing either to a bad translation, or design on the part of the writer, two distinct characters are so run together in the same sentence, that we would suppose them to be one person if we did not know that the person who leaned on the bosom of the Lord could not be the one who bore the sacerdotal plate, and was a martyr.

It would seem from this effort to make it appear that there were two Johns buried at Ephesus, that the philosophers proved that the John who bore the sacerdotal plate was the one the Christians were attempting to impose on the world as the real John, and that the proof was such that they had to yield the point, and claim that there were two graves—one the martyr's, and the other the Apostle's. Eusebius felt conscious that it was not safe to rest his case here, and we find him reaching out in every direction for further proof, satisfied with anything that will give color to the fact he labors to establish.

In another place he states : " Where it is also proper to observe the name of John is twice mentioned. The former of which he (Papias) mentions with Peter and James and Matthew, and the other apostles ; evidently meaning the evangelist. But in a separate point of his discourse he ranks the other John with the rest not included in the number of apostles, placing Aristion before him. He distinguishes him plainly by the name of Presbyter. So that it is here proved that the statement of those is true who assert there were *two* of *the same* name in Asia, that there were also two tombs in Ephesus, and that both are called John's even to this day; *which it is particularly necessary to observe.''* (Eusebius, *Ecc. Hist.*, book iii. chap. xxxix.) As much as to say to the objecting philosophers, If you have proved that one John in Asia was the Presbyter John, we prove by Papias that there were two, and that one of them was the Apostle. If this is so, it is only by inference. But it spoils the argument when it is shown that when Papias speaks of the two Johns, he does not say they were in Asia, or where they were. He speaks at the same time of all the Apostles, or nearly so, by name, but does not mention them, or any of them, in connection with any place. To subserve a particular purpose, Irenæus had asserted that John had been in Ephesus, where he remained a long time, without the least authority to sustain him. It was a bare, naked assertion without proof.

In the third and fourth centuries, during the

time of Eusebius, this assertion had grown to great importance, by reason that, on the fact that it was so, was founded the Apostolic succession of nearly all the churches in Europe, and most of Asia. To maintain the presence of John in Asia was as important as it was to prove that Peter had been in Rome. Understanding the importance of this fact, the philosophers directed their attacks upon it, showing that the man the Christians called the Apostle was somebody else. It devolved upon Eusebius, the most learned man of his day, to defend the position. The task exceeded his ability, but not his inclination to deceive. If we except Irenæus, no writer has so studiously put himself to work to impose falsehoods on the world as Eusebius, Bishop of Cæsarea. His genius was employed in various ways, and especially in perverting chronology. Speaking of a class of men who gave themselves up to such employments, the author of the " Intellectual Development of Europe," page 147, says : " Among those who have been guilty of this literary offence, the name of the celebrated Eusebius, the Bishop of Cæsarea in the time of Constantine, should be designated, since in his chronography and Synchronal tables he purposely 'perverted chronology for the sake of making synchronisms.' (*Bunsen.*) It is true, as Niebuhr asserts, ' He is a very dishonest writer.' To a great extent, the superseding of the Egyptian annals was brought about by his influence. It was forgotten, however, that of all things chronology is the least suited to be an object of inspiration, and that, though men may be wholly indifferent to truth for its own sake, and consider it not improper to wrest it unscrupulously to what they may suppose a just purpose, yet that it will vindicate itself at last." His character for truth stood no better among writers of the fifth century, for Socrates fairly charges that in his life of Constantine he had more regard for his own advancement than he had for the truth of history. (Book i. ch. 1.) A whole volume is devoted to display the virtues and exalt the character of a man who had murdered his son Crispus—his nephew Licinius—suffocated his wife Fausta in a steam bath, and who, to revenge a pasquinade, was with difficulty restrained from the massacre of the entire population of Rome.

5*

In another part of this volume we will have occasion to detect and expose the genius of this Father, in his attempt to create a chronology so as to give semblance to a list of men who never existed, but who were required to fill an important gap in the life of the church.   No fitter instrument could be found to help consummate the fraud conceived by Irenæus to impose a spurious John on the world than Eusebius of Cæsarea.

# CHAPTER VIII.

The Gnostics.—Irenæus makes war on them.—His mode of warfare.—The Apostolic succession and the object.—No church in Rome to the time of Adrian.—Peter never in Rome—nor Paul in Britain, Gaul, or Spain.—Forgeries of Irenæus.

BEFORE we approach the principal subject treated of in this section, it will be proper to say something of a sect or society which in its day took a leading part in the affairs of the world, but which has long since disappeared from history, and whose former existence is now only known to the careful reader. We refer to the Gnostics, who for the most part flourished in the second century. They were divided among themselves into more than fifty different sects. " The principal among them were known under the names of Basilidians, Valentinians, and Marcionites. They abounded in Egypt, Asia, Rome, and were found in considerable numbers in the provinces of the West. Each of these

sects could boast of its Bishops and congrega-
tions, of its doctors and martyrs, and instead of
the four Gospels adopted by the church, they
produced a multitude of histories, in which the
actions and discourses of Christ and his apostles
were *adapted* to their respective tenets."—(*Decline and Fall*, chap. xv. vol. I. p. 257.) They
supported their opinions by various fictitious
and apocryphal writings of Adam, Abraham,
Zoroaster, Christ, and the Apostles. They were
for the most part composed of Gentiles· who
denied the divine authority of the Old Testament, and rejected the Mosaic account of the
creation, of the origin and fall of man, and
claimed that a God was unworthy of adoration,
who for a trivial offence of Adam and Eve pronounced sentence of condemnation on all their
descendants. They adored Christ as an *Æon*,
or divine emanation, who appeared on the earth
to reclaim man from the paths of error and
point out to him the ways of truth ; but with
these opinions they mingled many sublime and
obscure tenets derived from oriental philosophy.
This divine *Æon* or emanation they considered was the Son of God, but was inferior to

the Father, and they rejected his humanity on the principle that everything corporeal is essentially and intrinsically evil. They agreed with the Christians in their abhorrence of polytheism and idolatry, and both regarded the former a composition of human fraud and error, and that demons were the authors and patrons of the latter.

As we have stated, the Gnostics for the most part sprang up in the second century and disappeared in the fourth and fifth, suppressed by a law of the Emperor Constantine. "The Emperor enacted a law by which they were forbidden to assemble in their own houses of prayer, in private houses, or in public places, but were compelled to enter the Catholic church. . . . . Hence the greater number of these sectarians were led by fear of consequences to join themselves to the church. Those who adhered to their original sentiments did not at their death leave any disciples to propagate their heresies, for, owing to the restrictions to which they were subjected, they were prevented from preaching their doctrines."—(Sozomen, *Ecc. Hist.*, book ii. ch. 32.)

Thus passed from history the Gnostics, "the most polite, the most learned and most wealthy of the Christian name." (*Decline and Fall*, chap. xv. vol. I. p. 256.) Such was the character of the men who, brought into collision with the orthodox Christians in the second century, became involved in the most violent and bitter struggles in which men were ever engaged. It was to defeat and destroy these men that Irenæus devoted the labor of a lifetime, that on their ruin he might erect the Catholic church. The undertaking was Herculean, but the means employed were well chosen, vigorously and tenaciously pursued, and its success is one of the most remarkable and exceptional cases in history of the triumph of cunning, falsehood, and fraud. The grand idea was, that Christ, the Son of God, was the founder of the church on earth, and that, at his death, the power to establish others after him he conferred on the Apostles, and upon no one else. As they might confer this power on others as they had received it from Christ, so these last could in turn do the same to those who followed them, and in this way continue the church through all time. This is what Irenæus calls the "Apostolic succession." A church which could not prove its connection with Christ through this Apostolic chain was no church at all, and it amounted to impiety and vile heresy for such a pretended church to undertake to explain or understand his gospel. Such a church has no relation to Christ, but with demons and evil spirits.

Irenæus found it much less difficult to show that there was no such succession in the Gnostic churches than he did in proving that it existed in his own. To do this, as we will show in another place, he was forced to introduce on to the stage the names of at least nine persons who, he claimed, had been Bishops of Rome, most of whom were mere myths and never had an existence, and those who had were never in Rome at all.

Christ, at his death, he further maintains, not only conferred on the Apostles the sole right to establish churches, but also imparted to them some divine knowledge or gifts which they on their death intrusted to the church as a special deposit for the benefit of all who yielded obedience to her authority. These precious gifts left with the church Irenæus compares to money or riches deposited in a bank by a rich man. But we will let him speak for himself: "Since, therefore, we have such proof, it is not necessary to seek the truth among others, which is easy to obtain from the church ; since the Apostles, like a rich man depositing his *money in a bank*, lodged in her hands most copiously all things pertaining to the truth ; so that every man, whosoever, *can draw* from her the water of eternal life.   For she is the entrance to life, and all others are thieves and robbers."   (Book iii. chap. 4, sec. 1.)   Having established the principal proposition by his mere assertion (which is his way of making history of all kinds), Irenæus next proceeds to show that the Gnostics could not trace any connection with a church founded by the Apostles.   "For prior to Valentinianus (he says), those who follow Valentinianus had no existence: nor did those from Marcion exist before Marcion ; nor, in short, had any of those malignant-minded people, whom I have above enumerated, any being previous to the initiators and inventors of their perversity."   (Book iii. chap. 4, sec. 3.)

The ancient Father has, so far, established two of his main propositions : first, that a church must derive its origin through the Apostles, or some one of them, to be genuine; and second, that there was no such connection in the churches of the Gnostics ; and it only remains to show that the church claiming to be orthodox had. He declines to point out the order of succession in all the churches, but consents to do it in the case of Rome, which, he says, according to tradition, derived from the Apostles, was founded and organized at Rome by the two glorious Apostles, Peter and Paul. (Book iii. chap. 3, sec. 2.) The church at Rome, founded by such great lights as Peter and Paul, Irenæus continues, should be regarded of the highest authority in the church, for, he says, "it is a matter of necessity that every church should agree with *this* church, on account of its pre-eminent authority, that is, the faithful everywhere, inasmuch as the apostolical tradition has been preserved continuously by those faithful men who exist everywhere." (Sec. 2.)

As Peter was selected to be head of the church, and Rome the capital of the Christian world, the scheme to establish a church on the ground of an Apostolic succession must fail, unless it can appear that Peter had not only been there at some time, but that he was also the founder of a church at the holy city.  A letter said to have been written by Clement, the third Bishop of Rome, is selected as the medium by which it is made to appear that Peter had been in Rome; and Irenæus took upon himself to show what he was engaged in while there.  At the proper place we will show that this Clement is a fiction, brought on the stage as a link in the Apostolic chain forged by the great criminal of the second century.

Now follows a forgery so apparent on its face, that it does not require the skill of an expert to detect it.

"But not to dwell upon ancient examples, let us come to those who, in these last days, have wrestled manfully for the faith ; let us take the noble examples of our own age.  Through envy, the faithful and most righteous pillars of the church have been persecuted even to the most dreadful deaths.  Let us place before your eyes the good Apostles.  Peter, by unjust envy, underwent not one or two, but many labors : and thus having borne testimony unto death, he went into the place of glory, which was due to him. Through envy, Paul obtained the reward of patience. Seven times he was in bonds; he was scourged; was stoned. He preached both in the East and in the West, leaving behind him the glorious report of his faith. And thus having taught the whole world of righteousness, and reached the fullest extremity of the West, he suffered martyrdom by the command of the governors, and departed out of this world, and went to the holy place, having become a most exemplary pattern of patience." (*Epistle I. of Clement to Corinthians*, sec. 5.) By the side of this extract we will lay a passage of Irenæus. Speaking of the writers of the Gospels, he says : " Matthew also issued a written Gospel among the Hebrews, in their own dialect, while Peter and Paul were preaching at Rome, and laying the foundations of the church." (Book iii. chap. 1.) Now, we assert with confidence, that the hand which penned the first passage wrote them both. It is not said in so many words, in Clement's letter, that Peter was in Rome, but it is to be inferred, as in the case of John at Ephesus. Irenæus seldom states anything which is positively untrue in direct language, but makes falsehood inferential. The passage we have quoted does not contain a single truth, except as it relates to Paul. Paul and Peter were never engaged together in laying the foundation of a church. They quarrelled in Damascus and could never agree. The doctrine of circumcision formed an impassable wall between them, and, as we will show, was never given up by Peter. Besides, it is not true that Peter had anything to do in laying the foundation of the church at Rome.

Christians, during the reign of Claudius in Rome, were too few in number and too poor to form a church, especially such an one as would require the office of a Bishop. Renan, in speaking of the church in the time of Claudius, says it was composed of a " little group––every one smelt of garlic. These ancestors of Roman prelates were poor proletaries, dirty, alike clownish, clothed in filthy gabardines, having the bad breath of people who live badly. Their retreats breathed that odor of wretchedness exhaled by persons meanly clothed and fed, and collected in a small room." (*Life of Paul*, 96.)

We have no reason to believe that at any time during the life of Peter was the church of Rome, if there was any church there at all, composed of different materials or greater in numbers than at the time referred to. What was there for a Bishop to do in such a crowd, or what was there to keep him from starvation? Christians engaged in riots growing out of the hostility between them and the Jews were driven from Rome by an edict of the Emperor Claudius, and did not return during his reign, which ceased in A.D. 54, when that of Nero commenced. In A.D. 58 they had not rallied, and at that time Rome was without a church. It was the practice in all cases with Paul to address Christians through the churches, where churches were established ; but his Epistle, in A.D. 58, to the Romans, is addressed not to a church, but "*to all that be in Rome.*" In his three years' imprisonment in that city, commencing in the spring of A.D. 61, he makes no mention of a church, nor does he during the second, which lasted from the summer or fall of A.D. 65 to the spring of A.D. 66. There is no proof that the historian can discover, worthy of his notice, that there was a church in Rome of any kind, even down to the time of Adrian, A.D. 117, and even later. We are overrun with traditions on this subject, the creations of the second century, to which the attention of the reader will be called when we treat of the twelve traditional Bishops named by Irenæus. Adrian, in the seventeeth year of his reign, knew so little about a Christian church, that he supposed the office of a Bishop belonged to the worship of the god Serapis. In a letter written by him from Alexandria, A.D. 134, to his brother-in-law Servianus, he says: "The worshippers of Serapis are Christians, and those are devoted to the god Serapis, who, I find, call themselves Bishop of Christ."

We will dismiss this part of the subject for the present, with the promise to return to it in a subsequent chapter, when it will be demonstrated that there was no Christian church in Rome until about the reign of Antoninus Pius.*

---

* See Appendix C.

Were Peter and Paul together in Rome at all? Paul went there in the spring of A.D. 61, for the first time, and remained until the spring or summer of A.D. 63. During this time he wrote four epistles, as follows:—to the Ephesians, Philippians, Colossians, and to Philemon, and, if we except the first, he closes them by naming the persons who are with him. He says nothing about Peter, nor does he mention his name, so far as we know, during the three years he was confined in Rome. That Paul should omit to mention Peter, one of the Apostles, in some of his letters, is the very best proof that he was not in Rome at all. After his release in the spring of A.D. 63, after making a visit to the churches in Europe and Asia, he returned to Rome again in the fall of A.D. 65. He had with him a few friends who stood by him to the last. They were Luke, Mark, Pudens, Linus, and Claudia. There could not have been many other Christians in Rome at the time besides those named, because Paul, after naming the above who sent salutations to Timothy, adds, "and all the other brethren," which implies that there were not many of them. Paul does not mention Peter, because he was not there.   Timothy, no doubt, was with Paul in the winter of A.D. 65 and A.D. 66, and was put to death in the spring of the latter year, with his friend and fellow-laborer.   We never hear of him again.   In the spring of A.D. 66, the labors and sorrows of the great Apostle of the Gentiles ceased.   He had fought the good fight—he had finished his work—he had *kept the faith;* and now, by his death, bore testimony to the doctrines he preached.   He was among the last of Nero's victims.   Nothing that belongs to history is surer than that Peter and Paul never were in Rome together, laying the foundation of a church, or anything else.

Having proved that one-half of what is stated by Irenæus in the passage which we have quoted is false, according to the usual rule for testing the truth of any statement, we might claim that the remaining half is also untrue.   But we ask no such advantage in disproving any of the statements made by this father.

*When* was Peter in Rome ?   No writer in the first or second century pretends to give the time when he was in Rome, or when he died.

Irenæus gives the names of twelve Bishops who succeeded each other, commencing with Linus, but does not give a single date, so that we can tell when or how long any one of them held the office. This want of dates, where it was easy to give them—if what was stated was true—was urged with so much force against what Irenæus said, that Eusebius, in the fourth century, undertook to fix the time when these traditional Bishops succeeded to, and how long each held the office. He fails to say when Peter first became Bishop, or when he ceased to be the head of the church, but commences giving dates from the time of Linus, his successor. Without intending, he has furnished the data to determine when Peter died, if his dates are correct, which is *not even probable.* He says : " After Vespasian had reigned about ten years, he was succeeded by his son Titus ; in the second year of whose reign, Linus, Bishop of the church of Rome, who held the office about twelve years, transferred it to Anacletus." (Eusebius, *Ecc. Hist.*, book iii. ch. 13.) As Linus succeeded Peter, the latter must have died just before his successor took the office. Titus became empe-

6

ror June 24th, A. D. 79, and as Linus died two years after this, after holding the office twelve years, he became Bishop in A. D. 69; which must have been the year of Peter's death. Nero died in June A. D. 68, and at his death the persecution against Christians ceased altogether. It is not claimed that Galba, Otho, Vitellius, Vespasian, or Titus ever inflicted persecution of any kind on Christians during the time they held the government of the empire. Eusebius, in attempting to fix a date when the second Bishop took office, answers the objections made to the vagueness of Irenæus, but robs Peter of the laurels of a martyr.

But it is claimed that Linus was installed Bishop before the death of Peter, and Irenæus pretends to give the time. He says: "The blessed Apostles then having founded and built up the church, committed unto the hands of Linus the office of the Episcopate." (Book iii. ch. 2, sec. 3.) The blessed Apostles are Peter and Paul. Now we have just shown that these Apostles were never in Rome together, and that there was no church to be committed to the charge of Linus or anybody else. As it is an important part of the story that Peter died a martyr at Rome, this could only happen to him between A. D. 64 and A. D. 68, for the persecution under Nero commenced during the former year, and ended with his death in A. D. 68. We have the most conclusive proof that Peter was not in Rome in A. D. 64, when the persecutions under Nero commenced, nor afterwards. He was in Babylon—whether Babylon in Assyria, Babylon in Mesopotamia or Egypt—he was in Babylon more than two thousand miles away. Peter was born about the time of Christ, and was sixty-four years of age when the persecutions under Nero began. He was married, and when he wrote his first Epistle he was in Babylon and had his family with him, for he mentions the name of Marcus, and calls him his son. " The church that is at Babylon, elected together with you, saluteth you ; and so doth Marcus, my son." (1 Peter v. 13.)

The date of this epistle is fixed by Dr. Lardner and other critics at A. D. 64. Did Peter, at the age of sixty-four, when he heard that Nero was feeding the wild beasts of the Amphitheatre with the flesh and bones of Christians,

" lured by the smell of blood," start for Rome ? If Peter was in Babylon in A. D. 64, an '' Apostolic succession," so far as it depends on him, must fail, and Rome must surrender the authority by which she has held the religious world in subjection for the last seventeen centuries.

But this she will never do, as long as her audacity and cunning are left to hatch schemes to escape from the dilemma. Inspired by despair, she now claims that Peter means Rome when he says Babylon, and that the Marcus spoken of was not the son of Peter, but the nephew of Barnabas and companion of Paul ! Just as well claim anything else, and say Babylon means Alexandria, and that Marcus was the stepson of Nero. Here two impressions are made : one that the letter was written at Babylon, and the other that Peter was attended by his son. Are both false ? What did Peter, or anybody else, expect to gain by giving false impressions ? By an agreement between Peter and Paul, made early and observed strictly, the labors of the former were limited to the circumcised, and he found them in large numbers in cities watered by the Euphrates. There and in Judea, among the Jewish people, was the scene of Peter's labors, and there he died. He had no business in Rome. As there was no church in Rome in A. D. 64, it is impossible, if Peter was there at the time, for him to make the salutation he does in his address to his countrymen. He could say, " the church that is at Babylon," but not " the church that is at Rome," for there was none.*

Mark the son of Peter, and Mark the nephew of Barnabas, are two different persons, whom the genius of Irenæus seeks to confound. The epistle to Philemon was written in the latter part of A. D. 63, which shows that Paul, Timothy, and Mark were then in Rome. They left in the following spring. During the winter of A. D. 63, Paul wrote the Colossians that they might expect Mark to visit them, and it would seem that he had made arrangements with them of some kind in regard to him, when he arrived among them. " Marcus, sister's son to Barnabas (*touching whom ye received commandments : if he come unto you, receive him.*") *Col.* iv. 10.

---

* See Appendix B.

Unless Mark changed his mind afterwards, he went from Rome to Colosse in Phrygia. The next reliable information we have of Paul after the spring of A. D. 63, except at Nicopolis in A. D. 64, he is back in Rome in the fall of A. D. 65, and in prison; and the first knowledge we have of Mark, he is in some part of Asia Minor. Timothy and Mark were together, and Paul writes to the former from his prison, to come to Rome and to bring the latter with him, and to get there before the winter sets in; which request was complied with. To suppose that Mark had been to Rome in the mean time would be most unreasonable, and against all the probabilities in the case. There was nothing to take him there until Paul called him back. If Peter was in Rome when he wrote his first epistle, in A. D. 64, Mark the nephew of Barnabas was not with him. If Mark saw Peter at all in A. D. 64, it was not in Rome. Nor did he see him that year in Babylon in Egypt, or Babylon in Mesopotamia or Chaldea.

The latter Babylon was long known for its vices and wickedness, and was called a sink of iniquity; and as Rome had become corrupt and steeped in crime of all kinds, it is claimed that Peter uses the word Babylon in a typical sense when he was writing from Rome !  If this is so, he did not write from Babylon in Egypt or Mesopotamia, as some have contended, for they were each small and inconsiderable places of no importance, and there could be no object in using either as a type to represent the corruptions of Rome.  If Mark saw Peter in Babylon, it was in Chaldea.  Measured by degrees of longitude, Rome and this Babylon are more than two thousand miles apart.  Why would Mark make a visit to Peter involving a journey of four thousand miles, or half that distance ? He never did.  He could not.  He went among the Colossians under some arrangement made by Paul, and no doubt remained with them until he was wanted at Rome.  When Peter calls Mark his son, he means just what he says. Mark the companion of Paul, and Mark the son of Peter, are two different men.

What should take Peter to Rome or keep him there when burning and torturing Christians was one of the amusements of Nero ?  Had Peter's character for courage so much improved that he went there when all the Christians had gone, to defy Nero, and invite his destruction ? There is something in the character of Peter that makes it improbable, if not impossible, that he should be in Rome in a time of danger. He was a man of strong impulses, but a constitutional coward. He followed Christ to the scene of the crucifixion, "but he followed him afar off." (*Matt.* xxvi. 58.) He had pride, and a proper sense of manliness, and when he was betrayed through a want of courage into the commission of a mean act, he had spirit and sense enough to be ashamed of it. He denied Christ, but it cost him bitter tears of repentance. Either his cowardice or his jealousy stood in the way of his coming to the aid of Paul, whenever Paul was in danger of his life. When the Jews were about to tear him to pieces in Jerusalem, and he had to be rescued by the Roman soldiers, Peter was nowhere about, and we do not even hear of him. In his trials before the Roman Governors, when he had no one to stand by him but a few faithful companions, the presence of Peter, at such a time, would have done much to aid and console the great champion of a common cause. But in all these places there was danger, and where danger was was no place for Peter.

He lacked moral, as he did physical courage. At Damascus he did not hesitate to sit at the same table with the uncircumcised, when there was no one present to object; but when those came from Jerusalem who could not tolerate the liberal ideas of Paul on circumcision, he cowardly sneaked away. Paul took fire at the appearance of so much meanness, and boldly reproved him. Is this the kind of man who would enter the lion's den, and brave the wrath of Nero at a time when the tyrant was flooding the streets of Rome with the blood of Christians?

Justin Martyr was born about the year A. D. 100, and was a native of Neapolis in Syria. (*Apology*, sec. 1.) At the beginning of the reign of Antoninus Pius he fixed his abode in Rome, and afterwards wrote numerous works, principally devoted to the defence of Christians. (Cave's *Life of Martyr*, vol. 2, chap. 6.) No one had better opportunities of knowing about Peter, and the church at Rome, than he had,

6*

and no one who wrote as much as he did which concerned Christianity, would have been more likely to mention him, if what Irenæus says of him had been true.   He is so oblivious of Peter that he seems to have been unconscious of his existence.   No writer in the first years of the second century, who is entitled to credit, speaks of him, and he first begins to figure in the pages of Irenæus when the disputes with the Gnostics were at their height.   The Clementines were composed later in the century, when Pauline Christianity was giving way to the new school, and the dogma of an Apostolic succession had taken possession of the church.   Diony-sius, Bishop of Corinth, who lived and wrote during the reign of Marcus Antoninus and his son Commodus, about A. D. 180, according to Eusebius, also states that Paul and Peter were at Rome together engaged in laying the foundation of a church.   (Eusebius, *Ecc. Hist.*, lib. ii. ch. 25.)   But this writer has got out of the Pauline period, and even goes beyond Irenæus, for he states, according to the same authority, that Peter and Paul laid the foundation of the church at Corinth.

Theophilus of Antioch, Melito of Sardis, Apollinarius of Hierapolis, all writers about the same time, A. D. 180, like Irenæus, take sides against the Gnostics, and show that they were committed to the new school. From this time Irenæus is quoted as the authority for the fact that Peter and Paul had founded the church at Rome, and we are asked to give special weight to what he says, as he was the companion of Polycarp, who had seen and conversed with John.

Speaking of Paul, Clement is made to say, " He preached both in the East and in the West —taught the whole world righteousness, and reached the farthest extremity of the West, and suffered martyrdom, by the command of the Governors." This passage has long been a stumbling-block among learned critics. It is the only authority on which is founded the story, that after Paul was discharged from prison in A. D. 63, he went into Spain, Gaul, and Britain. Caius, the Presbyter, in the beginning of the third century, says : " Writings not included in the canon of Scripture expressly mention the journey from Rome into Spain." Hippolytus, in the same century, says that

Paul went as far as Illyricum, preaching the gospel.  Athanasius, in the fourth century, says that St. Paul did not hesitate to go to Rome and Spain.  Jerome, in the same century, says that "St. Paul, after his release from his trial before Nero, preached the Gospels in the Western parts."  (Quoted from Chevallier's *Apostolical Epistles*, note, p. 487.)

There is no authority for Paul's travels in the Western provinces, except the passage from Clement, and as Irenæus is the founder of the story, it is not improved by the repetition of subsequent writers.  The whole is a transparent falsehood.  From the time of Paul's career, commencing with his adventure near Damascus to the time of his imprisonment in Rome, in the spring of A. D. 61, we have an account of his travels, and know where he was each year during this time.  He never in this time went west of Rome.  In the spring of A. D. 63, in company with Mark, Titus, Timothy and others, he left Rome and went in all probability to Colosse, where, in pursuance of some agreement he made with the people of that place, he left Mark. How long he remained is uncertain, but the next time we hear of him he is in Crete, where no doubt he spent the winter of A. D. 63 and A. D. 64. In the mean time he made some converts, whom he left in charge of Titus, and in the spring went west into Macedonia. Some time in the summer or fall of A. D. 64 we find him in Nicopolis, where he informed Titus he meant to spend the winter. The following spring or summer he went to Rome and was soon imprisoned. If he was at Colosse or Crete in A. D. 63, and Nicopolis in A. D. 64, he could not have gone to Britain, Gaul, and Spain between the spring of A. D. 63 and the summer of A. D. 65, for it would not be possible.

But it is conclusive that Paul did not go into the provinces of the West after his release from prison ; that there is no mention of his travels in the West, except what is said in this passage from the letter of Clement—a thing impossible, when we consider that he never went anywhere but he made his mark, and left his footprints behind him. Even Paul himself, in his subsequent letters, makes no allusion to any such travels, which is accountable upon no other hypothesis than that he never made them. But what was gained in fabricating this passage ?

The idea of Irenæus, that there could be no church unless its origin could be traced to some one of the Apostles, who were special bankers of divine favors, never left him. He furnished Rome with Peter, and Asia with John, and now he is required to furnish one for the churches in Gaul, Spain, and Britain. Here were churches in these countries in his day, and who had authority to establish them ? It would not do to claim that either of the Twelve had been in the West, for even falsehood has its boundaries. Paul will do. He is the great Apostle of the Gentiles. Besides, according to the Acts, he had submitted to ordination at the hands of the Apostles. The explanation of the reasons which dictated this spurious passage in Clement's letter is consistent with the acts of Irenæus, and the whole current of his thoughts throughout his life. But this story, invented by him, has been repeated by others, until it settled down— as history ! It is clear from the proof here shown, that Irenæus has no claim to our belief as a writer, and that the statements he makes in regard to Peter in Rome and Paul in the West are mere inventions of his own to assist him in his disputes with the Gnostics, in which he was engaged for the best part of his life.

# CHAPTER IX.



Irenæus, after stating that Peter and Paul preached in Rome and laid the foundation of a church at that place, continues: "After their departure, Mark, the disciple and interpreter of Peter, did also hand down to us in writing what had been preached by Peter. Luke also, the companion of Paul, recorded in a book the gospel preached by him." (Book iii. sec. 1.) Again no time is given. The last time we know anything of Mark and Luke that is certain, or at all reliable, they were both with Paul in Rome. In his second letter to Timothy he says: "Only Luke is with me. Take Mark, and bring him with thee: for he is profitable to me for the ministry." (2 *Timothy* iv. 11.) That Timothy obeyed this request and took Mark with him, does not admit of doubt. Paul and Timothy were inseparable, and Mark was Paul's near friend and companion. This must have been in the fall of A. D. 65, when Paul was in prison, with little or no hope to escape the second time from the fangs of Nero.

At the time Timothy and Mark entered Rome, the fury of Nero raged with all its sanguinary cruelty. It was just about the time the conspiracy of Piso was brought to light. Made mad by his fears, he struck in all directions. Not content with the destruction of the conspirators, he put to death all who offended his vanity or moved his jealousy. Seneca, a man whose many virtues added lustre to the Roman people, and who was an honor to any age, was not suffered to live. His very virtues gave offence to the tyrant. Lucan and others, distinguished for genius and learning, were put to death. Tacitus says that at this time " the city presented a scene of blood, and funerals darkened all the streets." (*Annals,* book XV. sec. 21.) Speaking of the events of the year 66, when Paul was put to death, the same writer says : " We have nothing before us but tame servility, and a deluge of blood spilt by a tyrant in the hour of peace. The heart recoils from the dismal story. But let it be remembered by those who may hereafter think these events worthy of their notice, that I have discharged the duty of an historian, and if in relating the fate of so many eminent citizens, who resigned their lives to the will of one man, I mingle tears with indignation, let me be allowed to feel for the unhappy. The truth is, the wrath of Heaven was bent against the Roman State. The calamities that followed cannot, like the slaughter of an army or the sacking of a city, be painted forth in one general draught. Repeated murders must be given in succession." (*Annals*, B. XVI. sec. XVI.) The author then proceeds to give a long list of victims. At the time Paul was in prison, and Mark and Luke his companions were with him, the Roman legions, under the command of Vespasian, were marching to make war upon the Jews, if they had not done so already. They had rebelled and defied the power of Rome. At this time, no Jew could be in Rome and live. Not only was the anger of Nero aroused against them, but that of the entire people of Rome—and this feeling did not abate until after almost the entire nation was destroyed. No doubt Timothy, Luke, Linus, Paul, and all others who were with them, perished in the general calamity. Why put to death Paul, and not his fellow-laborers? Nero waged war not against Christians, but against Christianity. We trace all these parties inside the gates of Rome, and then we lose their trail forever. There is not one single item of reliable proof that any one of them ever left the doomed city. The footprints of Christians going into Rome at this time were like the tracks going into the cave of Polyphemus—many were seen going in, but none coming out.

We learn from Eusebius and Jerome, that Mark went to Egypt and founded a church at Alexandria, and the latter states that he died and was buried there in the eighth year of the reign of Nero. This is impossible. As Nero commenced his reign A.D. 54, this would make him die in A.D. 62. Now we find him alive with Paul in A.D. 65. Eusebius, in his loose way, says: "The same Mark, *they say also,* being the first that was sent to Egypt, proclaimed the gospel there which he had written, and first established churches in Alexandria." (Book I. ch. 16.) This father had special reasons why he wanted to get Mark to Alexandria. The close resemblance between Christians and Therapeutæ, as we have shown, was a reason with him why he should insist that the latter were in fact believers in Christ by a different name. Mark is sent to be their teacher, and was claimed to be the founder of this new sect of Christians. Nothing is wider from the truth. If ever Mark or Luke left Rome, there is no reason why we should not hear something of them. Situated as they were in their relations with the founders of Christianity, had they survived the slaughter at Rome, one or both would have left behind them evidence, of some kind, of their escape. What remained of Paul, Timothy, Mark, Luke, Linus and others after they entered Rome in the winter of A.D. 55 and A.D. 66, could only be found after that time among the graves of Nero's victims. Whatever Mark and Luke wrote, in the nature of Gospels, was written before they entered the gates for the last time.

As this was in A. D. 65 or A. D. 66, and the gospels ascribed to them were neither extant nor known before the beginning of the second century, we are forced to look to some other quarter for those who wrote them.

But what proof is there that Mark and Peter were on such intimate terms as is claimed by Irenæus? None, except that which is afforded in the first Epistle of Peter (1 *Peter* v. 13), wherein Mark is spoken of by Peter as his son. What better evidence can we have of the studied dishonesty of Irenæus, than his attempt to have it appear or believed that the Mark referred to in the first of Peter, was the companion of Paul and interpreter of Peter? We have just shown he was not—but an entirely different person, and it sweeps away the whole foundation upon which rests the claim that the Gospel of Mark was written at the dictation of Peter. While Mark was with Paul, either in Rome or Asia Minor, Peter, with his son Mark, is preaching among the Jews of Chaldea.

What Presbyter John says on this subject is here worthy of notice. Eusebius, speaking of the writings of Papias, says: " He also inserted into his work other accounts of the above-mentioned Aristion respecting our Lord, as also the *traditions* of the Presbyter John, to which refer-ring those that are desirous of learning them, we shall now subjoin to the extracts from him already given a *tradition* which he sets forth concerning Mark, who wrote the Gospel, in the following words: ' And John the Presbyter also said this : Mark being the interpreter of Peter, whatsoever he recorded he wrote with great accuracy, but not in the order in which it was spoken or done by our Lord, for he neither heard nor followed our Lord, but, as before said, he was in company with Peter, who gave him such instruction as was necessary, *but not to give a history of our Lord's discourses.*' " (Eusebius, *Ecc. Hist.*, book iii. chap. 39.) Papias here gives *a tradition* derived through Presbyter John. Slender proof that Peter dictated the Gospel of Mark ! To rank among canonical Gospels, and as a corner-stone of Christianity, with the authority of an inspired book, the proof falls far below what we have a right to expect and demand. On such a subject it is no proof at all.

It is difficult to tell what Mark did write, according to Papias. What he did write was not in the order in which the events in the life of

Christ occurred—nor in the order in which he spoke or taught. Peter would not allow him to give the history of our Lord's discourses. If that is so, then the Gospel to which Papias refers is not our present Gospel of Mark. This relates the acts of Christ in the order of time, and gives his discourses in full. In this respect the second Gospel does not differ from the first and third. It is quite probable that Mark, in his intercourse with the Apostles, may have learned many things in relation to Christ which he wrote out, but which, like the Hebrew Gospel of Matthew, was condemned or cast one side, as it did not help to strengthen the new ideas in relation to Christ, which sprang up some time before the death of Paul. But we can never know what Mark wrote, as Papias does not claim he ever saw it, nor do we know of any one who did.

What is said by Clement of Alexandria and all other writers on the origin of the second Gospel is derived from the extract taken from the works of Papias, and from what is said by Irenæus: their statements do not better the case, any more than a superstructure will give strength

to the base on which it rests. If Mark ever
wrote anything, it would contain nothing that
did not accord with Paul, for he was not only
his fellow-traveller, but he was his fellow-laborer
in the spread of the doctrines of Christianity ;
and so near and dear were the relations between
them, that when Paul saw his end approach, he
wrote to Timothy to bring Mark with him, as
brother would for brother, for a parting interview.   What Paul taught, Mark believed—and
Paul dead or Paul in life would have made no
difference with Mark.

After reading the Gospel of Mark, who would
suppose that he had been the companion of
Paul and the interpreter of Peter ?  We would
expect to find some thought or expression that
had in it the soul of Paul, as his very spirit pen-
etrated all his followers and made them a reflex
of himself.   Paul drew from the depths of his
own consciousness, which he took for revelations, the ideas which formed the basis of his
religion and made Christ what he believed him
to be.   It was a holy faith with him, discon-
nected from all material laws.   The second Gospel is founded on works, and the divinity of

Christ proven by his power over the laws of the universe. All nature bows down before him; even demons and evil spirits fly before his presence. Mark the interpreter of Peter!! Where do we see Peter in the Gospel of Mark? What, all at once, has become of circumcision? Did he, after his quarrel with Paul, shake off his Jewish prejudice and bigotry and rise to a higher plane? The proof is he did not.

Paul, Luke, and Mark were as companions inseparable—they were fellow-laborers, held the same doctrines, died for the same cause and at the same time.

In another chapter we inquired from what source Luke got his knowledge of the wonderful statement he makes in relation to the visitation of the angel to Mary and Zacharias, for he did not get it from Paul, who never mentions the name of Mary. We now ask, from whom did Mark learn the story of John the Baptist? Paul knew nothing about him. Who had a better opportunity than he to know everything which related to him, if he had been the person described by Mark? What better proof can be offered to show that neither Luke nor Mark wrote the Gospels ascribed to them, than that theÿ are made to state matters which lay at the bottom of Christianity in after-ages, of which Paul, their teacher and co-laborer, knew nothing? To find the authors of these Gospels we must look to the second century.

# CHAPTER X.

Acts of the Apostles.—Schemes to exalt Peter at the expense of Paul.

THE Acts of the Apostles dates between A. D. 140 or 150 and A. D. 170. The book, *as we now find it*, was not in existence before Justin's *Apology*, because before his time there were no miracles, as will be shown; while the Acts abounds in them of the most extravagant character. Between A. D. 140 or 150, and A. D. 180, is the time when the war among the different sects raged with the greatest violence, and frauds and forgeries were practised by all parties without remorse or shame. It was during this time that Lazarus was made to rise superior to death, and assume his place among men, after his body had become putrid and began to decay. There was nothing too false or extravagant for parties to assert at this period of the world, and the only wonder is, that the absurd stories of the age have passed down to subsequent generations as truths of a revealed religion.

The book of the Acts, in its present form, came to light soon after the doctrine of the Apostolic succession was conceived, for it is very evident that the first half is devoted to give prominence to Peter among the Apostles, who was to be made the corner-stone of the Church. As all other churches are made to bow to the supremacy of Rome, so all the Apostles must be subordinate to Peter. This is so obvious that the work is overdone. On the day of Pentecost he is put forward to explain the miracle of the cloven tongue, and show that it was in accordance with what the prophet Joel had foretold—which if Peter did say what he is made to say, only proved his ignorance of what the prophet meant. His miraculous powers are wonderful. He cured a man forty years old, who had been lame from his birth, so that he leaped and walked. His power extends over death, and he raises Dorcas from the grave. He is now chief speaker. Ananias and his wife Sapphira fall down dead before him. So extraordinary is his power over diseases, " that they brought forth the sick into the streets, and laid them on beds and couches, that *at the least the shadow of Peter* passing by might overshadow some of them." (*Acts* v. 15.)

It is surprising that the incredulity of the Jews did not give way before such wonderful works; but it seems it did not, and the only effect produced on their minds was to send Peter to prison. Peter is twice committed to prison for doing good, and the sole object in sending him there is to give an opportunity to the Lord to deliver him, and show that he is under the special protection and guardianship of God. "And behold, the angel of the Lord came upon him, and a light shined in the prison; and he smote Peter on the side, and raised him up, saying, Arise up quickly. And his chains fell off from his hands. And the angel said unto him, Gird thyself, and bind on thy sandals: and so he did. And he saith unto him, Cast thy garment about thee, and follow me." (*Acts* xii. 7, 8.) "And when Peter was come to himself, he said, Now I know of a surety that the Lord hath sent his angel, and hath delivered me out of the hand of Herod, and from all the expectation of the people of the Jews " (verse 11).

The person over whom the Lord had manifested so much care, must certainly have been set apart to act some great part in his providences towards our race.  At the time we are writing about, the struggle between the followers of Peter and Paul was raging ; the latter claiming that the Apostle of the Gentiles was of equal authority as to doctrine with Peter or any of the Apostles ; while the former insisted that Paul had a special commission—to convert the 'Gentiles—and as he had performed his work, his mission ceased, and he was no longer to be regarded as an authority in the church.  No less a person than God himself can settle the dispute, and the cunningly devised stories of Cornelius, and Paul's conversion, are introduced into the Acts in order to give the Lord an opportunity to decide between the two parties.

Cornelius, a devout man, is laboring under what is called religious conviction, and is in doubt what to do.  He stands in need of a spiritual adviser, and when in this condition of mind, " He saw in a vision evidently, about the ninth hour of the day, an angel of God coming in to him, and saying unto him, Cornelius. And when he looked on him he was afraid, and said, What is it, Lord? And he said unto him, Thy prayers and thy alms are come up for a memorial before God. And now send men to Joppa, and call for one *Simon*, whose surname is Peter." (*Acts* x. 3, 4, 5.) The centurion was sent to Peter, because he was the depositary of divine light, and the dispenser of spiritual gifts—an intimation from God to all the world, for all ages, where men must look to, to find the true interpreter and expounder of religious faith. Cornelius did as he was commanded.

But it was not enough that this was true of Peter; but it must be shown that Paul was but a simple missionary, whose powers ended with his death. To do this, the story of his conversion in the Acts is told, notwithstanding it is in direct conflict with what Paul says himself on the subject. When Ananias was requested by the Lord to call on Paul while he was still prostrate from the effects of the blow he received near Damascus, he declined to do so—apparently in fear of Paul, on account of his previous treatment of Christians. This gave the Lord an opportunity to tell Ananias, why he is anxious to do as he was requested. "But the Lord said unto him, Go thy way : for he is a chosen vessel unto me, to bear my name before the Gentiles, and kings, and the children of Israel : for I will shew him how great things he must suffer for my name's sake." (*Acts* ix. 15, 16.)

The Lord has now settled all disputes between the followers of Peter and Paul, and the office of each is settled and defined. Under such a judgment, pronounced by God himself, no wonder the influence of Paul ceased to be felt in the latter part of the second century, and Peter proportionally increased in weight and authority. This attempt to put up Peter and put down Paul, determines the date of the Acts, and fixes it somewhere between A.D. 150 and A.D. 170, a period in the century prolific of spurious writings. It may be called the Petrine age of Christianity.

When Paul made his defence before the Jews at Jerusalem, and explained to them the mode of his conversion, it would be dangerous, or at least suspicious, to leave out the story of Cornelius ; but as it differed so much from the one he gives in second Corinthians, it was necessary to omit the one given in the epistle entirely. But the fraud is easily detected. The account as given in the Acts, to the sixth verse inclusive, is as it was doubtless delivered by Paul ; but from this point the story diverges from the one given by himself, and is a sheer fabrication. "And it came to pass, that, as I made my journey, and was come nigh unto Damascus about noon, suddenly there shone from heaven a great light round about me." (*Acts* xxii. 6.) Then according to Paul's account, given in his letter to the Corinthians, he was caught up to the third heaven, and there heard unspeakable words which it was not lawful for man to utter. What transpired between God and Paul, all took place in heaven, where no man could bear witness. The account in the Acts, which commences in the seventh verse, says that after the light shone from heaven, Paul fell to the ground, and did not ascend to heaven, but was led by the same light to Damascus. This version is to let in the story of Ananias. He could not bear witness

7*

to what passed between the Lord and Paul in the third heaven, but he might if the scene was laid on the earth. Besides, what passed between the Lord and Paul the latter does not pretend to state, for the words he heard were unspeakable and not lawful for man to utter. There is nothing in the story in the Acts that is unspeakable or unlawful to be repeated, unless it is to be regarded as a piece of blasphemy.

Had Paul told the story as given in the Acts in his defence, there was nothing in it to arouse the Jews to such a pitch of madness as to cause them to insist that he should be put to death. There was more in it to provoke a sneer than to excite anger. The scene in Jerusalem, when Paul was compelled to make his defence, was in A.D. 58, and he could have appealed to Ananias, who in the course of nature might still be living, and others, if the story was true. It was not the story in the Acts that incensed the Jews. When Paul claimed he was taken up to heaven, and there met the Lord and talked to him face to face, he had reached, in the minds of his hearers, a point in blasphemy that drove them to frenzy, so that they exclaimed : " Away with such a fellow from the earth : for it is not fit that he should live." The Jews listened to Stephen with patience until he exclaimed, " Behold, I see the heavens opened, and the Son of man standing at the right hand of God," when they could stand it no longer, and ran upon him with one accord and stoned him to death. It is clear that Paul's defence, made before the Jews, of his conversion, is omitted, and the story of Ananias substituted, to aid the enemies of Paul in placing Peter over him.

When we find the same story variously stated by Paul, and in the Acts, there should be no hesitation in choosing between the two. The Acts, like the works of the early fathers, bears so many marks of forgeries, to suit the emergencies and wants of the day, that very little contained in either is of any historic value. The epistles of Paul had obtained a large circulation before the time when the men of the second century inaugurated an era of forgeries, and long before the Acts were in existence ; so that the forgers were compelled to exercise great caution when they came to deal with the epistles, and only ventured to insert passages into the genuine writings to give the sanction of his name to the doctrines of the Alexandrian or Johannean school, or some dogma of the day. Such passages are scattered all through the epistles, but we can easily point them out, for they are doctrinal and exceedingly pointed.

Peter disappears at the end of the twelfth chapter; but enough has been done to make him chief among the Apostles, and claim for him a spiritual supremacy in all matters which relate to the church. John, afterwards the great light of Asia, only plays the part of an esquire to Peter, his lord and superior. They are often together, but John is not suffered to speak. It was designed that John, who was to take Asia in charge, should stand next to Peter; but the writer, by imposing silence on him on all occasions, took care that the supremacy of Peter was not put in jeopardy. The preaching of Philip in Samaria was a device to show that Peter and John were superior to the rest of the Apostles in their power to confer the Holy Ghost. Philip made many converts, both men and women, and he baptized them—but his baptism was not sufficient. " Now when the Apostles which were at Jerusalem heard that Samaria had received the word of God, they sent unto them Peter and John. They laid their hands on them, and they received the Holy Ghost."—*Acts* viii. 14, 17.

According to Paul, and this is made clear by the quarrels between him and Peter, as related in the epistles, the latter was tenacious to the last for the Jewish rite of circumcision, and we have no evidence, and no reason to believe, that he ever gave it up. A sectarian Jew would never answer to be the head and founder of a Catholic church. The sectarian character of Peter must be got rid of, and we see studied efforts in the Acts to do so. We have seen that Peter, in the first words he addressed to Cornelius, took the opportunity to declare that he believed in the doctrine that God was no respecter of persons. But this was not enough, in the opinion of the writer of the Acts, or at least the first half, and to make Peter's emancipation from his old Jewish opinions more conspicuous, and enable him to explain how it happened that the change was brought about, the vision of Peter on the house-top is produced. He went up upon the house-top to pray, about the sixth hour, and became very hungry ; but while they were preparing something for him to eat, he had a trance, " And saw heaven opened, and a certain vessel descending unto him, as it had been a great sheet knit at the four corners, and let down to the earth : wherein were all manner of four-footed beasts of the earth, and wild beasts, and creeping things, and fowls of the air. And there came a voice to him, Rise, Peter; kill and eat. But Peter said, Not so, Lord ; for I have never eaten anything that is common or unclean. And the voice spake unto him again the second time, What God hath cleansed, that call not thou common. This was done thrice : and the vessel was received up again into heaven."

The command of the Lord to Peter to eat, was a command to give up his Jewish views and notions ; for that all flesh was alike, and equally proper to be taken on an empty stomach. Peter was at a loss to understand the vision, and while he was revolving the subject in his mind, Corne-lius and his party came to be instructed by him, in accordance with the directions of the Lord. When Cornelius, who was of the Gentiles, made known the object of his visit, Peter at once understood the import of the vision, and exclaimed, "Of a truth I perceive that God is no respecter of persons," and that the gospel of Christ is to supply the spiritual wants of all nations, as the beasts and fowls are to furnish food for the hungry.

The conversion of Peter receives further importance and prominence from the defence he is compelled to make before the brethren, for his disregard of the rite of circumcision in the baptism of Cornelius. Peter makes a speech, in which he declares that he was commanded by God, not less than three times, to give up his old Jewish notions ; and no sooner was the command given than Cornelius, a Gentile, who was sent to him by God, made his appearance. The command from God to Peter, and the arrival of the centurion, who was instructed by the Lord to come to him, left him no choice in the matter, and that he baptized the Gentile, in obedience to the commands of the Lord. The reason was sufficient. "When they heard these things, they held their peace, and glorified God, saying, Then hath God also to the Gentiles granted re-

pentance unto life." (Acts. xi. 18.) The wall
between Jew and Gentile is now broken down,
and Peter a fit subject for the head of a universal or catholic church.

It seems that the person who put the speech
into the mouth of Peter, renouncing circumcision, was not satisfied with what he said at the
time. Something had been omitted or overlooked. Peter had shed his Jewish skin, but
the Lord had not given him a commission to
preach the gospel to all nations, and this he
must have to be the head of a universal church.
At the council held at Jerusalem by the Apostles to settle the question of circumcision, Peter,
according to the Acts, seizes the opportunity to
supply the omission: "And when there had
been much disputing, Peter rose up and said
unto them, Men and brethren, ye know how
that a good while ago, God made choice among
us, that the Gentiles, by *my mouth*, should hear
the word of the gospel, and believe." (*Acts* xv.
7.) Now there was no occasion for Peter to
make this claim or assertion, for it had nothing
to do with the subject before the council, and
was not true. The account which Paul gives

of what took place at the council is quite different, contradictory, and no doubt true. He
says, when he stated before the council the
trouble and vexations which were occasioned
by this rite, and reasons why it should not be
forced on the Gentiles, that Peter, James, and
John agreed with him—gave him the right hand
of fellowship, and then entered into a compact
that he should go to the Gentiles, and they to
the circumcised. (*Gal.* ii.)

This agreement was never departed from;
but not so with regard to circumcision. That
Peter, James, and all the disciples disregarded
the order of the Council in regard to that subject, is rendered clear by their subsequent conduct. After that, as much as two years, for
the Council was held in A.D. 49 or A.D. 50,
and the epistle to the Galatians was written in
A. D. 52, Peter went to Antioch, where he found
Paul. He ate with the uncircumcised until some
Jewish converts came from Jerusalem at the instance of James, who found fault with his course.
Peter, it seems, then changed front and stood
up for circumcision. " I withstood him to the
face," says Paul, for he was wrong. A discus-

sion springs up. Paul claimed that men were not to be saved through old rites and ceremonies, nor by works, but by faith. At this time, neither James nor Peter had given up their contracted notions on the Jewish rite. Nor had Peter as late as A. D. 57, twenty-four years after the death of Christ. Of the four parties which disturbed the peace of the church at Corinth at the time of Paul's first epistle to the Corinthians, which was written in A. D. 57, the party of *Cephas* was one. Peter was at the head of a party which held out for circumcision, seven years after the council at Jerusalem; and if he had not given it up then, when he was fifty-seven years old, there is no reason to believe he did after that. Nothing gave the men in the second century who undertook to put Peter at the head of a universal church so much trouble as this thing of circumcision, which we can readily detect by the pains and labors they have taken to free him from it. But the stain will not wash out.

The story told in the Acts about the way in which Peter was disenthralled from his narrow Jewish notions, is wholly inconsistent with the subsequent history of the church at Jerusalem. After the Lord had taken so much pains to prove to the disciples that a new dispensation had commenced, and the wall between the Jews and Gentiles was broken down, there was no reason why they should not all dispense with the practice of circumcision. But they never did. The fifteen first Bishops of Jerusalem, commencing with James and including Judas, were all circumcised Jews. (Eus., *Ex. H.*, B., iv. ch. v. Sulpicius Severus, vol. 11-31.) With the twelve disciples, jealousy of Paul, who fought this Jewish practice to the last, seemed to be the most active feeling of their natures, and we seldom hear of them unless they were dogging his footsteps, and stirring up the Jews against him. It was through their intrigues that the doors of the synagogue were slammed in his face wherever he went.

The doctrine of ordination, through which that deposit of divine riches which Irenæus says Christ left with the Apostles is made to flow in an uninterrupted current through all time, is conspicuously presented in the Acts. When Paul and Barnabas were at Antioch, and about to start for the West, on a mission to preach to

the Gentiles, the Lord said, "Separate me
Barnabas and Saul for the work whereunto I
have called them. And when they had fasted and
prayed, and laid their hands on them, they sent
them away." (*Acts* xiii. 2, 3.) Nothing could
impose so great a humiliation as this upon Paul.
The Lord again interferes and assigns him to a
special duty, and to make this humiliation complete, he is ordered to receive his commission at
the hands of the Apostles. Who laid their hands
on Barnabas and Paul, is not stated, nor is it of
any importance, as the object of the statement
is to make it apparent that the latter, the great
light of the Gentiles, submitted to the rite of ordination by the imposition of hands, administered by some one of the Apostles. Will any one
believe this story to be true ? If he does, he
does not understand the character of Paul.
There is nothing he would resent with so much
feeling, as he would such an admission on his
part that he was less than an Apostle. When it
was claimed he was not, his soul took fire, and in
his address to the Galatians, in the first chapter, he delivers himself in this defiant strain:
"*Paul, an Apostle, (not of men, neither by*

*man, but by Jesus Christ, and God the Father, who raised him from the dead.*) But when it pleased God, who separated me from my mother's womb, and called me by his grace, to reveal his Son in me, that I might preach him among the heathen; immediately I conferred not with flesh and blood : Neither went I up to Jerusalem to them which were Apostles before me." (Gal. i. 1, 15, 16, 17.) Is this the Paul who patiently submits to receive his commission from an Apostle to preach the doctrines of Christ to the nations of the earth at Antioch, when he is about to commence his labors?

It is not enough that Paul should submit to receive the Holy Ghost at the hands of the Apostle, and in this way be authorized to preach the gospel; but he gives the ordinance his full sanction by conferring ordination on others. " And it came to pass, that, while Apollos was at Corinth, Paul having passed through the upper coasts, came to Ephesus; and finding certain disciples, he said unto them, Have ye received the Holy Ghost since ye believed? And they said unto him, We have not so much as heard whether there be any Holy

Ghost. And when Paul had laid his hands upon them, the Holy Ghost came on them; and they spake with tongues, and prophesied." (*Acts* xix. 1, 2, 6.) No stronger proof could be given that the followers of Paul were opposed to the Episcopacy and the doctrine of succession and ordination, and contended against a government by Bishops with zeal to the last, than the labored and frequent efforts that are made to show that he himself gave his sanction to the order.

For Paul's persistence in claiming a human origin for Christ, there was a studied effort in the second century to destroy his claims as an Apostle; but after his epistles had undergone alterations so as to make Christ the Son of God in the sense of Philo, that is, who existed from all time, he was restored to favor, and his powers wonderfully magnified. He is now able to work miracles, and his power to heal diseases is such, that whatever comes in contact with his person, is so filled or imbued with holy energy, that its curative properties are sufficient to put death at defiance.

It is clear that the Acts of the Apostles is not the work of one century, but of two. The real itinerary of Paul commences in the thirteenth chapter, and from this to the end of the Acts, we can trace his footsteps in his various journeys among the churches, until he finally enters the gates of Rome, in the spring of A.D. 61.

## CHAPTER XI.

Matthew the author of the only genuine Gospel.—Rejected, because it did not contain the two first chapters of the present Greek version.

MATTHEW, surnamed Levi, was a native of Galilee. Before his conversion to Christianity he was a publican, or tax-gatherer, under the Romans, and collected the customs of all goods exported or imported at Capernaum, a maritime town on the Sea of Galilee, and received tribute paid by passengers who went by water. From the position of Matthew, he must have been a man of some learning and judgment, and from what we know of the early lives of the other Apostles, the only one among them, except perhaps Peter and James, that was capable of writing out a correct account of what was said and done by Christ.

As the first church at Jerusalem increased in number, and new converts were added to it, there was a necessity that there should be some written history given of what was said and taught by Christ before his death ; and as Matthew was in every way qualified, the task was imposed on him. Matthew wrote this book about A.D. 40, not much, if any, more than seven years after the death of Christ. Everything was fresh in his memory, and no doubt he was particular to give to the new converts a full and correct knowledge of all the doctrines taught by Christ, and especially to place before them his sermon on the mount, so full of divine morality, which was to form the soul of the new religion.

From all we know with certainty, this Gospel of Matthew was the only account of Christ in use among the members of the first Christian church, and their only means of information, except what they learned direct from the other Apostles. Everything, then, was just as it fell from the lips of Christ, and had the odor of fresh-gathered flowers. How the Christians at Jerusalem clung to this Gospel of Matthew, their sufferings and persecutions through a period of more than two centuries will bear witness. These Christians, afterwards called by

8

way of aversion Ebionites, were charged with the alteration of the Scriptures. This alteration, according to Epiphanius, consisted in the addition of the first two chapters of Matthew, which contain the account of the miraculous conception of Christ. The statements of Epiphanius are verified by the fact, that at the time these two chapters were added, by the men of the second century, we can trace through the pages of Ignatius, and other early fathers, numerous forgeries and interpolations which are unmistakable, and were intended to sustain the new aspect which Christianity took on in the early part of the second century. The addition of the two chapters, and the forgeries, belong to the period when the religion of Paul had passed off into the Philo-Alexandrian period of Christianity. Eusebius informs us what were the crimes of the Ebionites: "They are properly called Ebionites by the ancients, as those who cherished a low and mean opinion of Christ. For they consider him a *plain and common man*, and justified in his advances in virtue, and that he was born of the Virgin Mary by natural generation." (Eusebius, *Ecc. Hist.*, book iii. chap. 27.)

The views held by the Ebionites of Christ were derived from the Gospel of Matthew, and what they learned direct from the Apostles. Matthew had been a hearer of Christ—a companion of the Apostles, and had seen and no doubt conversed with Mary. When he wrote his Gospel everything was fresh in his mind, and there could be no object on his part, in writing the life of Jesus, to state falsehoods or omit important truths in order to deceive his countrymen. If what is stated in the two first chapters in regard to Christ is true, Matthew would have known of them ; and, knowing them, why should he omit them in giving an account of his life ? It was impossible to pass from the first to the second stage of Christianity, as long as the Gospel of Matthew was recognized as authority in the church. It stood as a mountain in the way, and had to be torn down and made way with. The history of the Ebionites, from the time they are charged with altering the Scriptures, to the time when they disappear from history, is one of tyranny and bloody persecution. In the reign of Adrian, what was left of them settled in the little town of Pilla, beyond the Jordan, from whence they spread themselves into villages adjacent to Damascus. Some traces of them can be discovered as late as the fourth century, when they "insensibly melted away; either into the church or synagogue." (*Gibbon*, ch. xv. vol. i. p. 255.) With them perished the genuine Gospel of Matthew, the only Gospel written by an Apostle.

Much useless labor has been bestowed on the question, whether the genuine Gospel was written in the Hebrew or Greek language. How this may be is of little consequence, since the genuine writing is no longer in existence. It is just as certain that the present version of Matthew was written in Greek, as that the genuine one was published in the Hebrew tongue. To the church of Rome the world is indebted for the destruction of the only genuine Gospel, and with it the only authentic account of Christ. No greater loss could befall the world. It was written in the dawn of Christianity, before corrupt and ambitious men sought to make religion a way to power and distinction. The truths contained in this Gospel stood in the way of a gigantic scheme, conceived by corrupt

and arrogant men, who saw in a church established by the authority of God, the road to the
highest point of human power and grandeur.
They succeeded, but their success,—

" Brought death into the world and all our woe."

It was not necessary to reject all of Matthew's
Gospel, and it is very evident that much was
retained—such as the discourses of Christ and
some portions of history.

# CHAPTER XII.

The character of Irenæus and probable time of his birth.
—His partiality for traditions.—The claim of the
Gnostics, that Christ did not suffer, the origin of
the fourth Gospel.—Irenæus the writer.

THE time when Irenæus was born is variously
stated. In the introduction to his works against
heresies, translated by Alexander Roberts,
D.D., and the Rev. W. H. Rambaut, A. B., is
the following passage on this subject: " We
possess a very scanty account of the personal
history of Irenæus. It has been generally supposed he was a native of Smyrna, or some
neighboring city in Asia Minor. Harvey, however, thinks that he was probably born in Syria,
and removed in boyhood to Smyrna. He himself tells us (lib. iii. sec. 3, 4) that he was in
early youth acquainted with Polycarp, the illus-
trious Bishop of that city. A sort of clue is
thus furnished as to the date of his birth. Dod-

well supposes that he was born as early as A.D. 97, but this is clearly a mistake, and the general date of his birth is somewhere between A.D. 120 and A.D. 140 (page 18).

Among the many strong and representative men who have impressed their genius on the Catholic Church, and given to it its distinctive features, none have equalled Irenæus, the Bishop of Lyons. It may in truth be said he was the father of the church. He assisted at its birth ; took charge of its infancy ; planted within its bosom seeds which sprouted and bore fruit which has been the source of its nourishment and strength for seventeen hundred years and more. It is enough to say of him, that he placed in the heart of the church the seed which bore the fruit of the Inquisition.

From the adoption of Trajan, in A.D. 98 to the death of the Antonines, in 180, a period of eighty-two years, has been selected by the learned author of the "Decline and Fall" as the most happy and prosperous period in the annals of the human race. (Vol. I. page 47.) The vast extent of the Roman Empire was governed by mild and just laws, administered by mild and just men. They respected not only the forms, but the spirit of a free constitution.

It was the prospect of peace and protection held out under this state of things that influenced the Christians who had survived the cruelties of other reigns to once more return to the imperial city. As soon as they were sufficiently numerous it was natural to adopt some form of government; but what that form was, we have no means of knowing, except by the dangerous light of tradition. It must be always fatal to tradition, where it claims to be important, that contemporaneous history says nothing about it. It is certain that the uninterrupted repose of the church, except in a few cases of persecution under Trajan, gave rise to disputes among Christians; for when they were relieved from the fears of an outward enemy, they soon found cause for quarrel among themselves. On the introduction of the three first Gospels, which happened during this time, as we shall prove, the character of Christ, or rather his mysterious birth from the Virgin, gave rise to numberless controversies.

Irenæus was born at the right time to be thrust into the midst of them, and as soon as he was able to comprehend anything, his ears were filled with the disputes of the various contending parties. He was born with a love of contention planted in him, and had the best school ever devised to cultivate and strenghten it. The character of his mind was bold and daring, and in support of the cause he espoused, he had no scruples or shame in resorting to falsehood and forgery. If the end was good, in his sight, it was all the same to him, whether it was reached by truth or its opposite. Such, indeed, was the prevailing morality of the age. Towards his adversaries he was bitter and vindictive, applying to them low and vile language, such as thieves and robbers. He claimed to look with contempt upon those who differed from him, and took pleasure in the repeated use of the word *heretic.* Whether he ever saw Polycarp or not, and it is no proof he did because he says so, he claimed great advantage from it, because, as he declares again and again, Polycarp was the disciple of the Apostle John. He is only one remove from an Apostle, and for what he states he claimed the weight of Apostolic authority.

We say again, it is very doubtful whether he ever saw Polycarp ; and it is very certain the latter never saw John. The studied dishonesty of Irenæus, in attempting to palm off the Presbyter John for the Apostle, is as dark a piece of knavery as is to be found in the history of a church which has encouraged such practices from the time it claimed to be the depository of all the divine wealth left by the Apostles.

Driven to the wall by the sharp logic and superior wisdom of that class of Christians who were distinguished by the name of Gnostics, his devious and ingenious mind undertook to cut them off from all claims as members of a Christian church, by interposing the doctrine of the Apostolic succession. This step once taken involved the necessity of repeated forgeries and frauds. Cowardly Peter is to be changed into a hero,—sent to Rome, where death is certain, and there die a Christian martyr. John, who had not life and force enough in him to rise above the masses, and no more knowledge than is wanted to dip a net into the sea, is to be converted into a fiery spirit, and put forth a book which is to fall like a thunderbolt on the heads of the heretics. If anything arises in the course of the debates, which, to ordinary men, would present difficulties, with Irenæus they were easily disposed of by tradition. He had traditions for all emergencies, and when his adversaries dared dispute him, he stands ready to silence them by abuse. He says : " But, again, when we refer them to that tradition which originates from the Apostles, (and) which is preserved by means of the successions of Presbyters in the churches, they object to tradition, saying that they themselves are wiser not merely than the Presbyters, but even than the Apostles, because they have discovered the unadulterated truth. It comes to this, therefore, that these men do now consent neither to Scripture nor to tradition. Such are the adversaries with whom we have to deal, my very dear friend, endeavoring like slippery serpents to escape at all points." (Irenæus, Vol. I. book iii. page 260.)

He brings often and repeated charges against his enemies for forgeries, and at the same time makes more himself than all of them put together. In the disputes about the twofold nature of Christ as he appears in the Synoptics, and as will be fully explained hereafter, the Gnostics had the advantage in the argument. If Christ the God descended upon the man Christ at the baptism in the Jordan, it left him at the crucifixion. Then, say the Gnostics, there *is no atonement*, for the Son of God did not shed his blood. No other man, in that or any other age, could meet the crisis but Irenæus; and the result is the fourth Gospel.

The time when this Gospel first appeared as a historical fact, has been so thoroughly sifted by late writers on that subject, that it will only be necessary here to notice some of the prominent reasons why its date is fixed after the middle of the second century. All allusions, or pretended allusions, found in the writings of the fathers, on inspection will be found to be the work of those who have attempted to poison the fountains of history. Papias lived near the age of John, and if John had written he must have known and spoken about it, as he speaks of Matthew and Mark; but he says nothing about John or Luke. He was Bishop of Heliopolis A. D. 165, and informs us that it was his habit to inquire of those who were the followers of the elders, what was said by them : what was said by Andrew and Peter or Philip ; what by Thomas, James, John, Matthew, or any other of the disciples of the Lord. (Eusebius, *Ecc. Hist.*, book iii. chap. 39.)

The Apology of Justin to the emperor was written some time between the years A. D. 130 and A. D. 160. The precise time is not known, and there is some uncertainty about it. In his Apology, Justin makes thirty-five distinct allusions to Matthew, eighteen to Luke, and five to Mark, and if he says anything which points to John at all, on examination it will appear that the allusions are found elsewhere, in writings anterior to Justin. "For Christ said, 'Except ye be born again, ye shall not enter into the Kingdom of Heaven.'" This, it is claimed, is taken from the fourth Gospel, which must have been in existence when Justin wrote. The language in the Gospel is, "Jesus answered and said unto them, Except a man be born again, he cannot see the kingdom of God." (*John* iii. 3.) This language, imputed to Christ, was drawn from a common source—from the Gospel according to the Hebrews, as has been fully proven, and so in every other instance where the writer seems to allude to the Gospel of John.

The new ideas concerning Christ found in this Gospel had not yet dawned upon the world when Justin wrote, for on that subject he had not got beyond what was contained in the Synoptics ; or, to speak with greater accuracy, his Logos idea was that of Philo, which differed from that of John.

An examination of this subject by the most learned and careful writers, proves that there is no reliable evidence that the fourth Gospel was in existence before A. D. 175, when a direct reference is made to it in the Clementine homilies, a production written in praise of Peter against Marcion. The language quoted is unmistakably the language of John. Tatian, who wrote between A. D. 160 and A. D. 185, quotes from the fourth Gospel : " And this is what was said, Darkness does not comprehend the light ; the Logos is the light of God." In the nineteenth chapter we read : " All things were made by

him, and without him not a thing was made."
These were quotations from John without his
being named as the author ; but Theophilus of
Antioch, who wrote about A. D. 176, especially
ascribes the Gospel to him. "In the second
book of this treatise addressed to Antolycus, he
says : 'Whence the holy Scriptures teach us,
and all who carried in them a holy spirit, of
whom John says, In the beginning was the
Word, and the Word was God.'" It may be
claimed as an historic fact, that the fourth Gospel
was extant in A. D. 175, and that all efforts to
give it an early date spring from uncertain
data : obscure allusions and doubtful inferences
altogether too vague and unreliable to satisfy
the mind in pursuit of truth.

## CHAPTER XIII.

Why Irenæus wrote the fourth Gospel in the name of
John.—He shows that the Gospels could not be less
than four, and proves the doctrine of the incarnation
by the Old Testament and the Synoptics.—The author of the epistles attributed to St. John.

THE zeal of Irenæus against his adversaries
had carried him so far in support of the doctrine
of the incarnation that he ventured upon a new
Gospel, under the name and authority of an
Apostle. Without the authority of some one of
the Apostles to sustain him, of what consequence would the opinion of one man be, on a
question which involved the substance and essence of Christianity? Nothing would be easier
than to publish a fourth Gospel in the name of
some one among the disciples. They were all
dead a hundred years or more, and the time
and place of their death no one knew.

But why did Irenæus select the name of John?
It was his policy to select from among the
twelve the one who had been the least conspic-

uous during his life, so that what was said or done by him in Judea at one time should not conflict with something else claimed to have been done at the same time somewhere else. The one that said and did nothing in his own country might be claimed to have said and done a great deal in another. If the proof adduced to prove that John, the son of Zebedee, was not the John of Ephesus, and that Irenæus was engaged in making a false substitute, we have gone a great way to show that he himself was the author of the fourth Gospel. To be sure, John's presence in Asia was required for the Apostolic succession; but the man who brought him there for that purpose would be most likely to use his name in all other cases when it might prove useful.

The book against Heresies was written between A. D. 182 and A. D. 188, so that about eight years elapsed between the appearance of the Gospel and the one against the heretics. In the mean time, no doubt the Gospel had been attacked from more quarters than one, so that it became necessary that the writer should come to its defence. The book against Heresies is nothing more than a supplement to the Gospel, and the writer had in view its defence as much, if not more, than he had the heresies of the Gnostics.

No better evidence could be given of the violence with which the fourth Gospel was attacked, when it first appeared, than the character of the defence made to sustain it. That it was something new in the time of Irenæus is evident from the fact that he is called upon and employed his genius to defend it. He is not called upon to defend either of the other Gospels, because whatever doubts there may have been as to them, the time for discussion had long passed away. But the fourth Gospel was something new; it had not gone through that fermentation in the minds of men which always follows the introduction of some new idea or principle, but was undergoing that process at the time Irenæus wrote in its defence. If this Gospel had been written by John, it would have been, at the time Irenæus wrote, over one hundred years old, and its claims settled years before he was born. The very arguments he brings to its support are proofs that it is a fraud. He proves that it is genuine because it is a necessity—just as pillars are necessary to the support of a portico. In his mode of argument he proves that a falsehood may be exposed by the poverty and weakness of the arguments which are relied upon for its support.

Irenæus proves not only that the appearance of the fourth Gospel was something new, but that the doctrines it contained were unheard of before. He says: "It is not possible that the Gospels can be either more or fewer in number than they are; for since there are four zones of the world in which we live, and four principal winds, while the church is scattered throughout all the world, and the pillar and ground of the church is the Gospel and the Spirit of life, it is fitting that she should have four pillars, breathing out immortality on every side, and vivifying men afresh." (Book III. chap. 2, sec. 8.) On this subject, after drawing many illustrations from the Gospels in proof of his position, he concludes as follows: "These things being so, all who destroy the form of the Gospel are *vain*, *unlearned*, and also *audacious:* those (I mean) who represent the aspects of the Gospel as being more in number than as aforesaid, or, on the other hand, fewer." (Book III. chap. 2, sec. 9.)

The fourth Gospel was written with no other purpose than to prove the incarnation, and that purpose is so persistently kept up in every line and verse, from the beginning to the end, that if we strike out this, and the miracles which are mere supports of the main idea, there is nothing left. And so with the third book against Heresies—it has but one theme. The writer sets out with the *Logos* idea of this Gospel, which is never lost sight of. He finds proof in the traditions of the church—in every page of the Old Testament--in the Synoptics, as well as in the fourth Gospel; and as we read his misapplication of words and sentences, we would conclude that he was a lunatic if we did not know he was something else. He has no quarrel with the three first Gospels, because he can see nothing in them that does not furnish proof of what is taught in the fourth ; and in the language which makes most against his dogmas, he sees the clearest proof of their truth.

As an example of his mode of interpretation, and turning the plain sense of words from their proper meaning to proofs that Christ was God in the flesh, we will give his explanation of the prophecy of Isaiah, which relates to his birth from a virgin: "Therefore, the Lord himself shall give you a sign: Behold, a virgin shall conceive and bear a son; and ye shall call his name Emmanuel. Butter and honey shall he eat: before he knows or chooses out things that are evil, He shall exchange them for what is good; for before the child knows good or evil, He shall not consent to evil, that he may choose that which is good." Here follow the comments: "Carefully, then, has the holy Ghost pointed out, by what has been said—His birth from a virgin and His essence, for he is God (for the name of Emmanuel indicates this). And he shows that he is a man when he says, ' Butter and honey shall he eat;' and in that he terms him a child also, in saying, ' before he knows good from evil;' for these are all tokens of a human infant. But that he ' will not consent to evil that he may choose what is good,' this is proper to God; that by the fact, that He shall eat butter and honey, we would understand that He is a mere man only—nor on the other hand from the name

Emmanuel, should suspect him to be Christ without flesh." (Book III. ch. 21, sec. 4.) That is, Christ is in the flesh, because he is to eat butter and honey ; and he is God, because he knows how to distinguish between good and evil ; and as a consequence, the divine and human nature are united in his person, and he is the incarnate God. We have shown in another part of this work that the prophecy of Isaiah had nothing to do with a future Christ, but was meant as a measure of time, governed by the period of gestation.

Again : " ' The Lord said unto my Lord, Sit Thou at my right hand, until I make thine enemies Thy footstool.' Here (the Scripture) represents to us the Father addressing the Son ; He who gave Him the inheritance of the heathen, and subjected to Him all his enemies. Since, therefore, the Father is truly Lord, and the Son truly Lord, the Holy Spirit has fitly designated them by the title of Lord. And again, referring to the destruction of the Sodomites, the Scripture says, ' Then the Lord rained upon Sodom and upon Gomorrah fire and brimstone from the Lord out of heaven.' For it here points out that the Son, who had also been talking with Abraham, had received power to judge the Sodomites for their wickedness. And this (text following) does declare the same truth : ' Thy throne, O God, is forever and ever ; the sceptre of thy kingdom is a right sceptre. Thou hast loved righteousness, and hated iniquity : therefore God, thy God, hath anointed thee.' For the Spirit designates both [of them] by the name of God—both Him who is anointed as Son, and Him who does anoint, that is, the Father. And again : ' God stood in the congregation of the gods, He judges among the gods.' He (here) refers to the Father and the Son, and those who have received the adoption ; but these are the church. For she is the synagogue of God, which God—that is, the Son Himself—has gathered by Himself. Of whom He again speaks : ' The God of gods, the Lord hath spoken, and hath called the earth.' Who is meant by God ? He of whom He has said, ' God shall come openly, our God, and shall not keep silence ;' that is, the Son, who came manifested to men, who said, ' I have openly appeared to those who seek me not.' " (Book III. chap. 6, sec. I.)

"And again, when the Son speaks to Moses, He says, 'I am come down to deliver this people.' For it is He who descended and ascended for the salvation of men. Therefore God has been declared through the Son, who is in the Father, and has the Father in Himself—He who is, the Father bearing witness to the Son, and the Son announcing the Father." (Book III. chap. 6, sec. 2.)

He quotes many passages from the Gospel of Matthew to prove his doctrine. "But Matthew says, that the Magi, coming from the East, exclaimed, 'For we have seen his star in the east, and are come to worship Him;' and that, having been led by the star into the house of Jacob to Emmanuel, they showed, by those gifts which they offered, who it was that was worshipped: *myrrh*, because it was He who should die and be buried for the mortal human race; *gold*, because He was a king, 'of whose kingdom is no end;' and *frankincense*, because He was God, who also 'was made known in Judea,' and was 'declared to those who sought Him not.'" (Book III. chap. 9, sec. 2.)  "And then, (speaking of His) baptism, Matthew says: 'The heavens were opened, and He saw the Spirit of God, as a dove, coming upon Him : and lo a voice from heaven, saying, This is my beloved Son, in whom I am well pleased.' For Christ *did not at that descend upon Jesus*, neither was Christ one and Jesus another : but the Word of God—who is the Saviour of all, and the ruler of heaven and earth, who is Jesus, as I have already pointed out, who did also take upon Him *flesh*, and was anointed by the Spirit from the Father—was made Jesus Christ." (Book III. chap. 9, sec. 3.)

The following is proof derived from Luke. " As Zacharias, also, recovering from the state of dumbness which he had suffered on account of unbelief, having been filled with a new spirit, did bless God in a new manner. For all things had entered upon a new phase, the Word arranging after a new manner the advent in the flesh, that He might win back to God that human nature (*hominem*) which had departed from God." (Book III. chap. 10, sec. 2.)

Many citations of a like nature are taken from Luke and Mark to prove the *Logos* doctrine of John's Gospel. Irenæus even brings John upon the stand to prove the doctrine of an incarnate Christ! which John himself was the first to communicate. "John, the disciple of the Lord, preaches this faith, and seeks, by the proclamation of the Gospel, to remove that error which by Cerinthus had been disseminated among men, and a long time previously by those termed Nicolaitans, who are an offset of that 'knowledge' falsely so called, that he might confound them, and persuade them that there is but one God, who made all things by His Word; and not, as they allege, that the Creator was one, but the Father of the Lord another; and that the Son of the Creator was, forsooth, one, but the Christ from above another." . . . . "The disciple of the Lord, therefore, desiring to put an end to all such doctrines, and to establish the rule of truth in the church, that there is one Almighty God, who made all things by His Word, both visible and invisible; showing at the same time, that by the *Word*, through whom God made the creation, He also bestowed salvation on the men included in the creation: thus commenced His teaching in the Gospel: ' In the beginning was the Word, and the

Word was with God, and the Word was God.'"
(Book III. chap. 11, sec. 1.)

He makes many references to John, and sums up his complaints against the Gnostics in the following words : " But according to the opinion of no one of the heretics was the Word of God made flesh.  For if any one carefully examines the systems of them all, he will find that the Word of God is brought in by all of them as not having become *incarnate* (*sine carne*) and *impassible*, as is also the Christ from above."
(Book III. chap. 111, sec. 3.)   The writer cites many passages from the epistle of Peter, all confirming the *Logos* doctrines of John. .

The following is the heading of chap. xxii. book III. : " *Christ assumed actual flesh, conceived and born of the Virgin.*"   In this chapter the doctrine of the incarnation is elaborately argued, and proof supplied from many quarters ; but as there is a great sameness in the argument throughout, it would only tire the reader to pursue the subject any further.·

The third book against Heresies contains twenty-five chapters, which are extended through one hundred and seventeen pages, and throughout there is but one idea presented, and the proof offered in its support; and from the first to the  last, there is a studied effort to turn the plain import of biblical passages from their true meaning into the support of the doctrines in the fourth Gospel.  Thus this father of the church, in about seven years after this Gospel appeared, came to its defence, and for that purpose wrote a book, which must have cost him much time and study, for in its way it is a work of great research, and required an intimate acquaintance with the Old and New Testaments, and the writings of the Gnostics, which were numerous in his day.  From the zeal which is shown throughout, it is evident that the writer had some personal interest in the subject, and that he was defending his own doctrines, and not those of St. John or any one else.

We do not detect in the work against Heresies the lofty and sublime tone of the Gospel, and, from the nature of the subject, it could not be expected.  He is engaged in an attempt to impose on the world, and as what he declares to be the work of an Apostle has no foundation in truth, nor the doctrines it teaches, he struggles like a man in a morass, who is compelled to seize upon anything to keep him from sinking. No doubt he was pressed hard by his adversaries, and he seems in his defence of the fourth Gospel like a gored bull with a pack at his front and heels. We can detect the keen lance of his adversary, piercing him to the quick, in the repeated cry of Antichrist, which is the favorite weapon when hard pressed by his enemies.

As he fights all his battles in the name of St. John, hear him exclaim, in the first and second epistles, which he falsely ascribes to the Apostle : " Little children, it is the last time : and as ye have heard that Antichrist shall come, even now are there many Antichrists ; whereby we know that it is the last time. Who is a liar but he that denieth that Jesus is the Christ ? He is Antichrist that denieth the Father and the Son." (1 *John* ii. 18, 22.) " Hereby know ye the Spirit of God : Every spirit that confesseth that Jesus Christ is come in the *flesh*, is of God : and every spirit that confesseth not that Jesus Christ is come in the flesh, is not of God. And this is that *spirit* of Antichrist, whereof ye have heard that it should come ; and even now

already is it in the world." (1 *John* iv. 2, 3.)
"For many deceivers are entered into the world, who confess not that Jesus Christ is come in the *flesh*. This is a deceiver, and an Antichrist. Look to yourselves, that we lose not those things which we have wrought, but that we receive a full reward. Whosoever transgresseth, and abideth not in the doctrine of Christ, hath not God. He that abideth in the doctrine of Christ, he hath both the Father and the Son. If there come any unto you, and bring not this doctrine, receive him not into *your* house, neither bid him God speed : for he that biddeth him God speed is partaker of his evil deeds." (2 *John* 7, 8, 9, 10, 11.)

The spirit that dictated the foregoing denunciations of those who disbelieved the dogma of Christ incarnate, also gave birth to what follows : "But again, those who assert that he was simply a mere man, begotten by Joseph, remaining in the bondage of the old disobedience, are in a state of death ; having been not as yet joined to the Word of God the Father, nor receiving liberty through the Son, as He does himself declare : 'If the Son shall make you

free, ye shall be free indeed.' But, being ignorant of Him who from the Virgin is Emmanuel,
they are deprived of His gift, which is eternal
life ; and not receiving the incorruptible Word,
they remain in mortal flesh, and are debtors to
death, not obtaining the antidote of life. To
whom the Word says, mentioning His own gift of
grace : ' I said, ye are all the sons of the Highest,
and gods; but ye shall die like men.' He
speaks undoubtedly these words to those who
have not received the gift of adoption, but who
despise *the incarnation* of the pure generation
of the Word of God, defraud human nature of
promotion into God, and prove themselves un-
grateful to the Word of God, who became *flesh
for them.*" (Book iii. chap. 19, sec. 1.)

## CHAPTER XIV.

Four distinct eras in Christianity from Paul to the Council of Nice.—The epistles of Paul and the works of the fathers changed to suit each era.—The dishonesty of the times.

FROM the time Paul commenced his labors, to the latter part of the second century, we can trace three eras or periods in the state and character of Christianity, as marked and distinct as the various strata of the earth which indicate the different ages of their formation. First, the Pauline ; second, the Philo-Alexandrian, which includes the time of the three first Gospels ; third, the Incarnation, which includes the fourth Gospel. As we approach the end of the third century, we may include a fourth period—that of the Trinity.

We have stated elsewhere, that the distinguishing feature between the Logos of Philo and the Christ of Paul was, that the former was coëxistent in point of time with the Creator or Father, while in case of the latter, there was a time he did not exist.   There was still another difference : the Logos was begotten in heaven, but Christ was born on the earth, of earthly parents. Through the influence of the Alexandrian Jews, who had been converted to Christianity by the preaching of Paul, the Christ of Paul was made to give way, in time, to the Logos of Philo. This change can be traced in the forgeries which are found interlarded through the epistles of Paul, and the writings of the early fathers. We trace the gradual and stealthy departure from the first to the second stages of Christianity in the use of terms in Paul's epistles which were employed among the Gnostics and others in the early part of the second century.   The epistles to the Ephesians and Colossians have been pronounced by able critics to be spurious, because of some verses which have an Alexandrian look ; when it is easy to discover that these verses are mere insertions into the original text. The term *pleroma*, or *fulness*, was a favorite phrase among the Gnostics, and now we find it scattered here and there through the epistles : " For it pleased the Father, *that in him* should all fulness dwell." (*Col.* i. 19.)   "For in him

9*

dwelleth all the *fulness* of the Godhead bodily."
(*Col.* ii. 9.) "And hath put all things under
his feet, and gave him to be the head of all
things to the church, which is his body, the
fulness of him that filleth all in all." (*Eph.* i.
22, 23.) "And to know the love of Christ,
which passeth all knowledge, that ye might be
filled with all the fulness of God." (*Eph.* iii. 19.)

The preëxistence of Christ, and his rank as
God, is now openly avowed. "For by him were
all things created, that are in heaven, and that
are in earth, visible and invisible, whether they
be thrones, or dominions, or principalities, or
powers : all things were created by him, and for
him. And he is before all things, and by him
all things consist." (*Col.* i. 16, 17.) Here the
Christ of Paul disappears, like the great Apostle himself. The works of the fathers are now
mutilated by the same ruthless hand, to maintain the new phase which Christianity is forced
to assume. "Ignatius, who is called Theophorus to the church which is at Ephesus in
Asia, deservedly happy, being blessed through
the greatness and *fulness* of God the Father, and
*predestinated before the world began,* that it

should be always unto an enduring and un-changeable glory; being united and chosen, through actual suffering, according to the will of the Father and Jesus Christ our God, all hap-piness by Jesus Christ and his undefiled grace." (*Epistle to Eptsiceris*, sec. 1. 17.)   The balance of this section, which will be cited in a subse-quent page, was added in the third or fourth cen-tury, when Christianity put on its fourth phase.

" For this cause they were persecuted also, being inspired by his grace, fully to convince the unbelievers that *there is one God*, who hath man-ifested himself by Jesus Christ his Son, who is his *eternal Word*, not coming forth from *silence*, who in all things was well pleased in him that sent him."؛ *   (Sec. 8.)

---

* The word *silence* is a word which grew in use among the Gnostics long after the time of Ignatius, and affords unmistaka-ble proof of the fraudulent interpolation.  Valentinianus, a Gnos-tic of the second century, held that there is a certain Dyad (two-fold being), who is inexpressible by name, of whom one part should be called *Anhetus*, unspeakable, and the other *Silence*. The word, in the connection in which it is found in the passage from Ignatius, speaking about what related to a later age, has been the occasion of much discussion : some contending that it has reference to the *Silence* of Valentinianus, which proves the

Such passages as we have cited, and others of a like nature which might be cited, have led critics to the conclusion that the writings which contain them are forgeries ; but if examined in *connection with the texts*, it will be found that they are interpolations, forced into the places they fill. As the writings of Paul now stand, they present Christ in two distinct characters or aspects : his own as the Son of Man, from which he never wavered ; and the other that of Philo. All through his epistles we find passages which inculcate doctrines with which he combated during his whole life. All that is essential to, or that is embraced in, the writings of Philo, as to the nature of the Logos, may be found in the epistles of Paul. We will give a few examples which we gather from the work of Jacob Bryant, and found among the notes of Adam Clarke in his Commentaries on St. John.

PHILO. " *First begotten of God.*"

COLOSSIANS i. 15. " Who is the image of the invisible God, the first-born of every creature."

---

passage spurious; others, that it relates to the erroneous opinions of heretics anterior to Valentinianus. What heretics ! (See Chevalier's *Apostolical Gospels*, note 6.)

HEBREWS i. 6. " And again, when he bringeth in the first begotten into the world, he saith,
And let all the angels of God worship him."

PHILO. " *By whom the world was created.*"

HEBREWS i. 2. " Hath in these last days
spoken unto us by his Son, whom he hath appointed heir of all things, by whom also he
made the worlds."

1 CORINTHIANS viii. 6. " But to us there
is but one God, the Father, of whom are all
things, and we in him ; and one Lord Jesus
Christ, *by whom are all things*, and we by *him*."

PHILO. " *The most ancient of God's works,
and before all things.*"

2 TIMOTHY i. 9. " Who hath saved us, and
called us with an holy calling, not according to
our works, but according to his own purpose
and grace, which was given us in Christ Jesus
before the world began."

PHILO. " *Esteemed the same as God.*"

PHILIPPIANS ii. 6. " Who, being in the form
of God, thought it not *robbery* to be equal with
God."

PHILO. " *He unites, supports, preserves, and
perfects the world.*"

Coloss. i. 17. " And he is before all things, and by him all things consist."

Philo. " *Free from all taint of sin, voluntary and involuntary.*"

Hebrews vii. 26. " For such an high priest became us, who is holy, harmless, undefiled, separate from sinners, and made higher than the heavens."

Philo. " *The Logos the foundation of wisdom.*"

1 Corinthians i. 24. "But unto them which are called, both Jews and Greeks, Christ the power of God, and the wisdom of God."

Coloss. ii. 3. " In whom are hid all the treasures of wisdom and knowledge."

Philo. " *Men being freed by the Logos from all corruption, shall be entitled to immortality.*"

1 Corinthians xv. 52, 53. " In a moment, in the twinkling of an eye, at the last trump : for the trumpet shall sound, and the dead shall be raised incorruptible, and we shall be changed." " For this corruptible must put on incorruption, and this mortal must put on immortality."

Inconsistency cannot be claimed to be one of

the faults of Paul ; but if we place these passages by the side of those in which he declares, in
unmistakable language, his belief in the nature
of Christ, we must either admit inconsistency
or fraud. The influence of Paul had lost much
of its force before his death in A.D. 66 ; and
when Hadrian assumed the government of the
empire, A.D. 117, the Pauline era had nearly
ceased. Speaking of the great Apostle, Renan
says : " After his disappearance from the scene
of his apostolic struggles, we shall find him soon
forgotten. His death was probably regarded as
the death of an agitator. The second century
scarcely speaks of him, and apparently endea-
vors to systematically blot out his memory.
His epistles are then slightly read, and only regarded as authority by rather a slender group."
(*Life of Paul*, page 327.)

But the same author tells us, on the same
page, what history confirms, that Paul, in the
third century, wonderfully rises in the estimation of the church, and resumes the place from
which he had been deposed. There is a good
and obvious reason for the change. During this
interval between the fall and rise of his influence,

his epistles had been subjected to the most glaring forgeries, in order to make them conform to the Philo-Alexandrian ideas which in the mean time prevailed.

It is to be remarked at this place, that the Logos idea of Philo encountered difficulties, when applied to the person of Jesus. It could not be denied that he was the son of Mary; but it might be, that he was not the son of Joseph. He is therefore born not of man. The influence of a divine energy is substituted. No sooner is this new feature introduced into the second stage of Christianity, than new forgeries commence, and are found scattered through the works of the fathers. " And the princes of the world know not the virginity of Mary, and him who was born of her, and the death of the Lord: three mysteries noised abroad, yet done by God in silence." " Where is the wise and where is the disputer ? Where is the boasting of those who are called men of understanding ? For our God, Jesus Christ, was born in the womb of Mary, according to the dispensation of God." (*Ignatius to Eph.* secs. 18, 19.)

The foregoing are mere specimens. Christ is

now the Son of God ; but for a time he is all humanity. He grows from infancy to manhood, and manifests in himself the appetites and infirmities which belong to the flesh. His mind develops early ; but, as with other mortals, it grew and expanded as he advanced in years. But the time came when "the heavens were opened unto him, and he saw the Spirit of God descending like a dove, and lighting upon him." (Matt. iii. 16.) He was there proclaimed by a voice from heaven, to be the Son of God. Here is something Paul never heard of. The new Logos of the gospel, like the Logos of Philo, was without beginning, from everlasting ; but from this point they diverge.

The Logos of the Alexandrian was not an *hypostasis*, or a person, but a divine emanation or spirit ; of a nature unconceivable, which hovered over the earth, but never touched it. The new Christ descended from heaven as a spirit, took up its mysterious abode in the human form, where it dwelt until its ministry was complete, when, with the body which contained it, it encountered death—went down into the grave— but on the third day broke the chains of death, and triumphantly ascended into heaven, from whence it came.

The tendency of the minds of men at that day towards the discussions of metaphysical and unintelligible subjects, soon led to endless disputes, growing out of this new feature of the Christian faith. How this mysterious union of God and man could and did exist, and when and how it was dissolved, were questions which caused much angry feeling and acrimonious discussion among Christians, which continued through the second, and even to the fourth century, when, according to the learned author of the " Decline and Fall," they died out by " the prevalence of more fashionable controversies, and by the superior ascendant of the reigning power." (*Gibbon*, vol. I. p. 257.)

The idle and profitless disputes of the second era of Christianity were forced, at a later day, to give way to those of the third. Cerinthus, and other Gnostics, maintained that the Son of God descended on the day of baptism in the form of a dove, and remained in its human receptacle until the time of the crucifixion, when it took its flight, leaving to the human form all the agonies and sufferings of death. If this were so, there is no atonement: the Son of God has not offered himself as a sacrifice. The Gnostics had the advantage of consistency. If Christ was a creature, like other men, when the Spirit descended upon him, and existed apart from the flesh, then death could only reach the body, and when that was put to death, or about to be, and the Spirit lost its tabernacle or abiding-place, it must again return to the celestial abode.

The perplexities and interminable disputes, caused by such unintelligible subjects, at last led to the third period in the Christian religion: the doctrine of the *incarnation*: "The *Word* was made flesh and dwelt among us, who was not born of blood, nor of the will of man, but of God." (*John* i. 13, 14.) God took upon himself the form of man, and was God in man. The Logos of Philo has become an hypostasis, and walks upon the earth. The war with the Gnostics has changed ground. The Son of God did not come down and take up his abode in the mortal form of Christ, but was Jesus himself, and when he came to suffer death there was no separation of divine and human natures, but the real Son of God shed his blood, suffered, and died on the cross as a sacrifice for the sins of our race.

The paternal solicitude of Irenæus in support of this new phase of Christianity is conspicuously displayed in the third book of his work against Heresies. "But, according to these men, neither was the Word made flesh, nor Christ, nor the Saviour (*Soter*), who was produced from [the joint contributions of] all [the Æons]. For they will have it that the Word and Christ never came into this world; that the Saviour, too, never became incarnate, nor *suffered*, but that he descended like a dove upon the dispensational Jesus; and that, as soon as He had declared the unknown Father, He did again ascend into the Pleroma. . . . Therefore the Lord's disciple, pointing them all out as false witnesses, says: 'And the Word was made flesh, and dwelt among us.'" (Chap. xi. sec. 3.) "As it has been clearly demonstrated that the Word, who existed in the beginning with God, by whom all things were made, who was also always present with mankind, was in these last days, according to the time appointed by the Father, united to His own workmanship, inasmuch as He became a man liable to suffering, [it follows] that every objection is set aside of those who say, ' If our Lord was born at that time, Christ had therefore no previous existence.'  For I have shown that the Son of God did not then begin to exist, being with the Father from the beginning ; but when He became *incarnate*, and was made man, He commenced afresh the long line of human beings, and furnished us, in a brief, comprehensive manner, with salvation ; so that what we had lost in Adam—namely, to be according to the image and likeness of God—that we might recover in Christ Jesus." (Chap. xviii. sec. 1.)

The forgers are again at their work.  The ancient fathers must be made to subscribe to the new creed.  " For some there are who are wont to carry about the name of Christ in deceitfulness, but do things unworthy of God, whom you must avoid as ye would wild beasts.  For they are raving dogs, which bite secretly, of whom you must be aware, as men hardly to be cured. There is one physician, both carnal and spiritual, create and increate, God *manifest in the flesh ;* both of Mary and of God ; first capable *of suffering*—then liable to suffer no more." (*Ignatius to Eph.* sec. 7.) "For whosoever confesseth not that Jesus Christ is *come in the flesh* is Antichrist ; and whosoever confesseth not his *sufferings upon the cross* is from the devil. And whosoever perverts the oracles of God, he is the first-born of Satan." (*Polycarp to Philippians*, sec. 7.)

The above citations are a few of many others of a like character scattered through the works of the fathers, inserted long after their death, and evidently intended to combat the idea of Cerinthus and others, that Christ did not suffer on the cross, and so it could not be claimed that by his death he made an atonement for the sins of man. Both of these fathers lived near the time of Paul, and believed the doctrines he preached : " Ye are the passage of those that are killed for God ; who have been *instructed in the mysteries of the gospel with Paul*, who was sanctified and bore testimony even unto death, and is deservedly most happy ; at whose feet I would that I might be found when I shall have attained unto God, who through all his epistles makes mention of you in Christ." (*Ignatius to the Ephesians*, sec. 12.) "For neither can I, nor any other such as I am, come up to the wisdom of the blessed and renowned Paul, who being amongst you, in the presence of those who then lived, taught with *exactness* and *soundness* the word of truth; who in his absence also wrote an epistle to you, unto which, if you diligently look, you may be able to be edified in the faith delivered unto you, which is the mother of us all." (*Polycarp to the Philippians*, sec. 3.)

Paul taught that Christ was born of woman, under the law; and Ignatius, that he was "truly of the race of David, according to the flesh." (*Letter to the Eph.*, sec. 1.)

The letters of Polycarp and Ignatius seemed a kind of a free commons where forgeries might be committed by all; and they have been so often used for this purpose, in order to secure the authority of their names to the doctrines of the day, that there is very little of the originals left. All parties were engaged in the practice; and each charged his adversary with doing the very thing that he was doing himself.

As we read whole pages in Irenæus, charging his adversaries with forgeries and false interpolations, we smile at the impudence and audacity of the man, who has done more to pollute the pages of history than any other, and whose foot-prints we can follow through the whole century, like the slime of a serpent.

Speaking of the forgeries of this century, Casaubon says: " And in the last place, it mightily affects me to see how many there were in the earliest times of the church, who considered it a capital exploit to lend to heavenly truth the help of their own inventions, in order that the *new* doctrine might be more readily allowed by the wise among the Gentiles.   These officious lies, they were wont to say, were devised for a good end ; from which source, beyond question, sprang nearly innumerable books, which that and the following age saw published by those who were far from being bad men (for we are not speaking of the books of the heretics), under the name of the Lord Jesus Christ and of the Apostles, and of other saints."   (*Casaubon*, quoted by Lardner.) Lardner is forced to admit " that *Christians of all sorts* were guilty of this fraud—indeed, we may say it was one great fault of the times." (Vol. IV. page 54.)

In an age where falsehood was esteemed a merit, the truth cannot be expected.  Before we close what we have to say on the third period of Christianity, we cannot fail to notice what a wide gulf has grown up between the religious faith of Paul and his followers, and those who gave their assent to the doctrines of the fourth Gospel.  But, wide as is the gulf, those who call themselves Christians can stand on the opposite banks and clasp hands as believers in a common faith.  Why is this?  Skilful artisans, in the second century and subsequent ages, have been busy in bridging over this vast abyss, by adding to and taking away from what Paul taught, until to cross over is neither difficult nor dangerous.

10

## CHAPTER XV.

**The Trinity, or *fourth period* of Christianity.**

IF we may judge of the opposition made to
the doctrines of the fourth Gospel by the vehe-
mence and bad feeling with which they were de-
fended, we conclude that if they were not successfully refuted, they did not escape just and
severe criticism. The sudden change from the
Logos of Philo to the *hypostasis* of John—from
Christ a spirit who had descended from Heaven and taken up a temporary abode in the human form, and a Christ who was born a God,
lived and remained such through death and the
resurrection—was too great a change to be suddenly taken, without provoking the sneers and
animadversions of the enemies of the new faith,
who were on the lookout to expose its weak-
nesses, and ridicule its inconsistencies. What
gave force and point to their attacks was, that
the change from the Logos of the Synoptics to
that of the fourth Gospel was one of necessity,

forced upon Christians by the tactics of the
Gnostics, in order to maintain a principle which
lay at the foundation of their religion : that is,
the atonement.

In the war waged between them and their
enemies, Christians found it a source of great
relief and satisfaction, to learn that the doctrines of John's Gospel, which were announced
in the first verses of the first chapter, were in
harmony with the theology of Plato. Whatever
inconsistencies might be imputed to them on
account of the change of their ideas as to the
nature of Christ, their present views were the
same as those held by the great philosopher of
Greece, whose wisdom had entitled him to be
called Plato the Divine. The study of the works
of the Athenian by Christians of this period
was the natural result of this feeling, and we
discover a constant increase of this admiration
until his ascendency is complete, and the nature
of the Godhead determined by his genius. The
followers of Plato were no less gratified to find
that the doctrines of the fourth Gospel were in
harmony with the school of their great teacher ;
so much so that it removed the prejudice, and

reduced the distance which formerly separated them from the Christians.*

According to John, the *Word* existed with the Father from the beginning—was equal to the Father, and was the Creator of all things. The Father, the Son, and the Holy Ghost were co-equal and co-eternal. With Plato, the Father, or First Cause, the Logos, and Spirit of the Universe, existed from the beginning, and were endowed with co-ordinate powers; but, according to him, all divine natures flow from the One, or First Cause, as light flows from the sun, and are bound in unity, and are one; so the three persons in the Godhead of Plato are one, and constitute a triad in unity.

The theology of the fourth Gospel approached so near to that of Plato, that it was natural that one should insensibly run into the other, and was what might have been expected. The Father, Son, and Holy Ghost are equal, as the First Cause, the Logos, and the Spirit of the

---

* Some proofs of the respect which the Christians entertained for the person and doctrines of Plato, may be found in *De la Mothe le Vager*, tom. V. p. 135, and *Basnage*, tom. IV. p. 29–79. *Decline and Fall*, vol. I. p. 440, note 29.

Universe are equal. As the two proceed from the One, or First Cause, with Plato, and are united, so the two proceed from the Father, and are one, and in both cases form a trinity in unity.

The circle is now complete. Paul was dethroned by the Alexandrian Philo, and his Christology in turn is overthrown by the mixed theology of John and Plato. We can readily detect the violence done the works of the fathers, in order to give the authority of their names to this new phase of Christianity. " Wherefore come all ye together as to one temple of God— as to one altar—as to one Jesus Christ—*who proceeds from One Father, and exists in one and is returned to One.*" (*Ignatius to Magnesians,* sec. 7.) This language expresses the Platonic idea in all its completeness. It could hardly be expected that Christianity could take upon itself this new phase without opening the door for new causes for dispute, as will always be the case when men presume to reason on spiritual generation, and from negative ideas attempt to draw positive conclusions.

Sabellius, of Egypt, undertook to find a middle ground, and while he admitted the triad in unity, he claimed that there was but one person in the Godhead, and that the *Word* and *Spirit* are only virtues or emanations of the Deity. But his doctrine conceded too much to the theology of the Greek to suit the followers of Arius, and not enough to satisfy the orthodox ; and so, after a vain struggle, Sabellius and his doctrines were swallowed up and lost sight of in the strife created by the opposing views which suddenly sprang up in the church at Alexandria. We give the origin of the dispute in the words of Socrates, a writer of the fifth century.

" After Peter, Bishop of Alexandria, had suffered martyrdom under Diocletian, Achilles was installed in the Episcopal office, whom Alexander succeeded, during the period of peace above referred to. He, in the fearless exercise of his functions for the instruction and government of the church, attemped one day, in the presence of the presbytery and the rest of his clergy, to explain, with perhaps too philosophical minuteness, that great theological mystery, *the Unity of the Holy Trinity*. A certain one of the Presbyters under his jurisdiction, whose name was Arius, possessed of no inconsiderable logical acumen, imagining that the Bishop entertained the same view of this subject as Sabellius the Libyan, controverted his statements with excessive pertinacity, advancing another error which was directly opposed indeed to that which he supposed himself called upon to refute. ' If,' said he, ' the Father begat the Son, he that was begotten had a beginning of existence : and from this it is evident, that there was a time when the Son was not in being. It therefore necessarily follows, that he had his existence from nothing.' " (*Ecclesiastical History*, book i. chap. 5.)

From a little spark, continues the writer, a large fire was kindled, which ran throughout all Egypt, Libya, the upper Thebes, and finally through Asia and Europe. After disturbing the peace of the world for fourteen hundred years, the dispute which commenced at Alexandria remains unsettled to this day.

We now approach a new era. Up to this time the religion of a people had no connection with the powers of the State. Constantine is the first to set an example. Indebted to the Christians for their assistance in the civil war

between himself and Licinius, under the pretext
of preserving the peace of the church, he wrote
an epistle to Alexander and Arius, admonishing
them to forbear and cease to quarrel about
things they can neither explain or comprehend.
Thus commenced a connection between church
and State which has proved so ruinous to the
cause of true religion, and the peace of the
church ever since.  This interference was continued by Constantine throughout his reign, and
at the time of his death the affairs of the church
and State were so interwoven that it became
difficult, at times, to distinguish between the office of a Bishop and the powers of the Emperor.

The spirit of faction in the church proved superior to the authority of Constantine, and in
order to restore peace, he was forced to call an
assembly of Bishops, Presbyters, and Deacons
from every part of the Christian world.  What
was meant to restore harmony, only furnished
fresh subjects for dispute, so that the progress of
mankind has rather been retarded than assisted
by the piety and wisdom of the Nicene fathers.
The attempt to fix a standard of faith by the
decrees of councils has proven to be the great-

est folly in which men were ever engaged, as it has been the source of the greatest misery and suffering ; and proves, by the evils which flow from it, that all such efforts are vain and presumptuous. As well undertake to fix a standard for the fine arts, and determine by a decree the combination of colors, and how the lights and shades shall be mingled in making a picture to please the eye, and satisfy the taste of all.

That which followed what was done at the Council of Nice, shows of what little value are the decrees of such bodies in establishing or in assisting the cause of truth. Council followed council, without arriving any nearer to the settlement of the dispute. In the fourth century alone, there were forty-five councils ; of these, thirteen decided against Arius, fifteen in his favor, and seventeen for the Semiarians. (Draper's *Intellectual Development*, page 222.) The divisions and quarrels among Christians sapped the strength, and finally led to the disruption of the Roman empire, and prepared the way for the armies of Persia, and the conquest of Mahomet.

10*

# CHAPTER XVI.

### The Catholic Epistles.

THE Catholic Epistles, as they are called, if genuine, should be regarded as of the highest authority in everything which relates to the early age of Christianity. That some are the real productions of an Apostle, some so in part, and others wholly spurious, is susceptible of the most satisfactory proof. The epistle of James, and the first of Peter, if we except certain parts of the latter, have strong claims to be treated as the works of the writers whose names they bear; while the second of Peter, the first, second, and third of John, and the one ascribed to Jude, carry on their face unmistakable marks of forgery.

The writer of the first epistle of Peter was a Jew, not a Greek, and it was addressed to Jewish converts. His mind dwells on events in Jewish history, for he speaks of Sarah, Abraham, and Moses, and refers to the traditions ol the Jewish rabbins and elders. (1 *Pet.* i. 18.) Although addressed to *strangers*, the epistle was meant for Jews, who, through persecution in Judea, fled into foreign countries; for to Peter was committed the ministry of the circumcision. (*Gal.* ii. 9.) Besides, the persons to whom Peter writes *are styled " a chosen generation, a royal priesthood, a holy nation*, a peculiar people" (1 *Peter* ii. 9), which can only apply to the Jewish nation. "And ye shall be unto me a kingdom of priests, and a holy nation." (*Exodus* xix. 6.)

The letter shows that Peter was still a Jew, and altogether proves that he had not changed his views on circumcision. The vision on the house-top had not yet taken place. But there is a spirit of pure morality running through the greater part of the epistle, which brings it near the time of Christ, and makes it out of place in a later period of Christianity. It is conclusive proof of its canonical authority, that it is inserted in the Syriac version of the New Testament, executed at the close of the first or early in the second century; and it is equally conclusive against the second of Peter, that it is not included in the same work. Hermas has not fewer than seven allusions to the first epistle, which is sufficient to prove its antiquity.

This epistle was also written before the order of Bishops was recognized in the church, and Christians had not departed from their first simple ideas of ecclesiastical government. Peter himself claimed to be nothing more than elder. "The elders which are among you I exhort, who am also *an elder.*" (1 *Peter* v. 1.)

The place where the letter bears date corresponds with our ideas of the movements of Peter, for his labors, whatever they may have been, were confined to Asia, not far beyond the confines of Judea.

But if the first of Peter is in the main genuine, it did not escape corruption at the hands of the poisoners of truth in the second century. "Who verily was fore-ordained before *the foundation* of the world, but was manifest in these last times for you." (1 *Peter* i. 20.) "Forasmuch then as Christ hath suffered for us in the *flesh*, arm yourselves likewise with the same mind: for he that hath suffered in the *flesh* hath ceased from sin." (1 *Peter* iv. 1.) When these verses were written, Christianity had passed into its third period, for here is announced *a Christ* who was co-eternal with the Father, and was *incarnate.*

Most of the first chapter, if not all, is undoubtedly spurious. The boastful spirit with which it commences ; the doctrinal announcements, and the tone in which they are delivered are entirely different from that shown in the following chapters. It is written as something to be used against an adversary, and, like all forgeries inserted into genuine writings for such purposes, much is crowded into a small space.

In this chapter is declared the preëxistence of Christ, or the Alexandrian Logos ; the resurrection ; foreknowledge and election, and sanctification—all disputed points in theology, which required the authority of an Apostle to settle : but neither of which had anything to do *with Christ or the religion he taught.* It will be noticed, that the crucifixion is mentioned twice : once in connection with the twentieth verse, which asserts the eternity of the Logos, and the other in close connection with the second verse, which holds to the doctrine of election. As the preëxistence of Christ was no part of Christianity when Peter wrote, which was, according to Lardner and others, in A.D. 64, but belongs to a later period ; and as the subject mentioned in the twentieth and twenty-first verses is the same, and cannot be separated, it follows that both are spurious.

So we would say of the mention of the resurrection in the third verse. It is connected with a doctrinal point which had no existence in Peter's time, and, if it had, was in dispute, and was inserted into this chapter to give it Apostolic authority. The mention of the resurrection in the twenty-first verse of the third chapter holds also a suspicious connection with the doctrine of baptism.

The true commencement of this epistle will be found in the first verse of the second chapter. Here we discover quite a different spirit. Here commences the plain, simple and pure doctrines of the Christian faith, which in the end will secure the victory. Peter and James are each examples to prove that a mind wedded to a single idea, which had for ages entered into the religion of a people, may be contracted and fettered by it, and yet be free to expand under the influence of the true genius of Christianity, and become liberal on other subjects. Neither Peter nor James could shake off the Jewish notion of circumcision, for it began with the father of that people by the command of God, and was to be binding on his descendants to the end of time. With them, like all the laws of God, the law of circumcision was unchangeable. But notwithstanding all this, they each had heart enough to take in the great truths of Christianity as declared by the lips of its founder. These men, who were slaves to one idea, who dogged the footsteps of Paul because he taught the doctrine of the uncircumcision, could yet teach men the duty to " love thy neighbor as thyself." (*James* ii. 8.)

No two writings can be more unlike than the two epistles ascribed to Peter. The second is filled with the boasting and controversial bitterness of the times of the Gnostics. In the primitive churches the authenticity of this epistle was a subject of doubt. It was not, as stated, included in the Syriac version of the New Testament, which cannot be accounted for, except that it was not in existence when it was compiled, at the beginning of the second century. But the internal evidence furnished by the epistle itself is sufficient to prove that it never was written by Peter.

The following contains the spirit of Irenæus when he speaks of his intimacy with Polycarp: " And this voice which came from heaven *we heard, when we were with him* in the holy mount." (2 *Peter* i. 18.) " But there were false prophets also among the people, even as there shall be false teachers among you, who privily shall bring in damnable heresies, even denying the Lord that bought them, and bring upon themselves swift destruction." (2 *Peter* ii. 1.) " And through covetousness shall they with feigned words make merchandise of you : whose judgment now of a long time lingereth not, and their damnation slumbereth not." (Chap. ii. 3.) " But these, as natural brute beasts, made to be taken and *destroyed*, speak evil of the things that they understand not; and shall utterly perish in their own corruption. . . . Spots they are and blemishes, sporting themselves with their own deceivings while they feast with you." (Chap. ii. 12, 13.) " For it had been better for

them not to have known the way of righteousness, than, after they have known it, to turn
from the holy commandment delivered unto
them. But it is happened unto them according
to the true proverb, The dog is turned to his
own vomit again ; and, The sow that was washed
to her wallowing in the mire." (Chap. ii. 21,
22.) The letter is filled with all the venom and
bitterness of the Gnostic quarrels.

We have already said enough to prove the
two epistles of John spurious, and who it was
that wrote them. " That which was from the
beginning, *which we have heard*, which we
*have seen with our eyes*, which we *have looked
upon*, and our *hands have handled*, of the Word
of life ; for the life was manifested, and *we
have seen it*, and shew unto you that eternal
life which was with the Father, and was manifested unto us." (1 *John* i. 1, 2.) Irenæus,
in a letter to Florinus, says, in speaking of Polycarp : " Well, therefore, could I describe the
very *place* in which the blessed Polycarp sat and
taught ; his going out and coming in ; the whole
tenor of his life ; his *personal appearance ;* the
discourses which he made to the people. How

would he speak of the conversations which he
had held *with* John and others who had *seen the
Lord.*     How did he make mention of their
words, and whatsoever he *had* heard from them
respecting the Lord."    All this he can say without a blush ; although Polycarp never saw John,
and in all his letters, which are numerous, he
never claims he did.    He saw Paul, but not
John.    The manner in which John is made to
speak of Christ is much the same as Irenæus
makes mention of Polycarp.    Effect is meant to
be given to what was stated in both cases, by
dwelling on details.

After having qualified himself as witness in
this boastful spirit, he proceeds to deal out
blows on the heads of his adversaries : " He
that saith, I know him, and keepeth not his
commandments, is a *liar*, and the truth is not
in him."    (1 *John* ii. 4.)    " Who is a liar but
he that denieth that Jesus is the Christ ?    He is
Antichrist, that denieth the Father and the
Son."    (Chap. ii. 22.)    " Every spirit that
confesseth that Jesus Christ is come in the *flesh*,
is of God : and every spirit that confesseth
not that Jesus Christ is come in the *flesh*, is not

of God." (Chap. iv. 2, 3.) Such is the spirit throughout the two epistles ascribed to John. The Apostle is forced on the stage to make war on the Gnostics, and maintain the dogma of the incarnation in the language of a blackguard.

The epistle of Jude is nothing but a bolt hurled at the heads of the Gnostics, from the hand of one who assumed the name of an Apostle.

What is said of the first epistle of Peter may be said of that which is attributed to James. It was written by a Jew, for he says: "Was not Abraham our father justified by works, when he had offered Isaac his son upon the altar?" (*James* ii. 21.) The text shows it was written during the Pauline period of Christianity, and was the work of James, or some one else, in reply to Paul, who claimed that faith without works were sufficient for salvation. It makes no allusion to the disputed dogmas of the second century, and like the first of Peter, breathes a spirit of Christianity which approached near the time of Christ. The frequent allusions to it by Hermas are in favor of an early date : it is included in the Syriac ver-

sion, which leaves its antiquity without question.

We cannot fail to be struck with the fact,
that Peter and James, both Jews, who were the
disciples and companions of Christ, are free
from doctrinal dogmas, and preach doctrines
like those of their Great Teacher, full of charity, kindness, and love.  It is only when we
come to the writings and forgeries of the
Greek that we encounter subtle and unintelligible dogmas, which involved men in endless
disputes, excited the most violent passions, and
terminated in wars and disturbances of all
kind.

What is remarkable, too, neither of these
Jewish writers makes any reference to the Gospels, nor to the miracles or prodigies spoken of
in them ; nor does either make mention of the
miraculous conception and birth of Christ.  All
these things sprang from the Greeks.  To be
sure, Paul preached the resurrection ; but he
believed because he saw Christ after the crucifixion, in a *vision*.  James is silent on the
greatest event since the creation, of which,
if true, he was a witness.  The hand of the

spoiler failed to leave his mark on the pages of James the son of Alpheus. Addressed to the "Twelve tribes which are scattered abroad," the epistle which bears his name had obtained too wide a circulation, and was in the hands of too many, before the age of forgery commenced, to be an easy subject for mutilation. It was written in Judea, and addressed to the whole Jewish people. It was for them alone, and in their special custody, and if it comes down to us without a spot or stain, as it came from the pen of the writer, it is because it was too well guarded and protected by its friends to admit of corruption. Why did James withhold from the twelve tribes the great fact that Christ had risen from the dead ? He speaks of his cruel death ; why not mention the still more important fact, that he rose superior to the grave, and put death under his feet ? "Ye have condemned and killed the *just ;* and he doth not resist you." (*James* v. 6.)

# CHAPTER XVII.

No Christians in Rome from A. D. 66 to A. D. 117.


FROM the death of Paul in A. D. 66, as we have before stated, to the reign of Adrian in A. D. 117, Rome was without a Christian population. Such is history when properly rendered. The course of Nero filled them with horror, and at the time of his death Rome was deserted by them. After he ceased to reign there followed the civil wars, the most fearful in the annals of Rome. Galba, after all obstacles in his way to power had been removed by the sword, entered the city through a scene of blood, and men expected nothing less than the renewal of all the cruelties of Nero's reign." (*Annals of Tacitus,* Appendix to book xvi.) Then commenced the civil war between Vespasian and Vitellius, which was the cause of untold misery to the Roman people. The city of Rome was burned to the ground. "From the foundation of the city to that hour, the Roman people had felt no calamity so deplorable, no disgrace so humiliating." (*Tacitus*, book iii. sec. 22.)

The condition of the times is truly depicted in the concise and eloquent language of the author of the "Decline and Fall:" "During fourscore years (excepting only the short and doubtful respite by Vespasian's reign) Rome groaned beneath an unrelenting tyranny which exterminated the ancient families of the Republic, and was fatal to almost every virtue and every talent that arose during that unhappy period." (Vol. I. page 47.)

Obscene rites alleged to be practised by Christians; their indifference towards all who differed from them in their ideas on religion; their isolation from the rest of mankind, had excited the hatred of the Pagan world; so that in large cities, where the population was lawless and difficult to restrain, they were liable to be attacked and torn to pieces without notice and without provocation. All the evils which befell the empire were referred to the Christians, and were regarded as proof that the Roman people had, by tolerating them, incurred the anger of heaven. Their presence was considered a curse upon the earth. Tertullian exclaims : " If the Tiber rises against the walls of the city, or the Nile does not overflow its banks; if there is a drought, or earthquake, or famine, or pestilence, the cry at once is, Take the Christians to the Lion." (*Apology*, chap. xl.)

It was this state of feeling that made it dangerous, especially during the civil war, for Christians to remain in Rome. Domitian, the son of Vespasian, commenced his reign in A. D. 81, and was assassinated in A. D. 96. That we have no account of any Christians being put to death under his reign is proof that they had not returned from the provinces. It is the fashion with historians to allege great cruelty towards Christians during this reign. We have searched for the evidence, but have failed to find it. Suetonius lived during his reign ; had personal knowledge of many things he describes ; gives the names of numerous victims and their offences ; mentions the cruelties inflicted on the Jews ; but does not even make use of the word Christian, or give the name of any one who suffered on account of his religion. The cruelty of Domitian spent itself on those who were guilty of political offences; but the interested and partisan traditions of the second century delight to make him a monster who took pleasure in shedding Christian blood. He did not fail to persecute Christians because he had no inclination to do so—for he punished what he called impiety to the gods with severity—but because there was none in Rome during his reign to persecute.*

Trajan succeeded to the empire in A. D. 98. During his reign, which continued to A. D. 117, what proof there is on the subject tends to show that Christians had not yet returned to the capital. So little did Trajan know about them, that Pliny, in writing to him for advice as to how he should deal with them, is compelled to describe to him their doctrines, practices and forms of worship. Had there been any in Rome at the time, there would have been no necessity for this; and besides, had there been any there, the mode of treatment of them by the emperor would afford a precedent for Pliny without calling for special instructions. But we can affirm

---

* See Appendix D.

I I

with confidence that no Christian dared live in Rome during this reign, which continued for nineteen years, for the reason that to be one during this time was a crime punishable by death.

In answer to Pliny's letter, in speaking of Christians, Trajan writes : " If they be brought before you, and are convicted, let them be *capitally* punished, yet with this restriction, that if any one will renounce Christianity and evince his sincerity by supplicating our gods, however suspected he may be in the past, he shall obtain pardon for the future on his repentance."

It is not at all astonishing that Pliny, in writing Trajan about his mode of treating Christians, had to tell him who they were, and describe the way in which they conducted themselves. From A.D. 64, when Tacitus speaks of them in connection with the great fire, and their sufferings at the time, no historian makes any mention of them, as dwellers in Rome, to the end of the century. The obscure allusion to them by Juvenal and Martial, in a satirical vein, relates solely to their conduct under torture, inflicted by Nero at the time Rome was burned.

Suetonius, who was secretary to the Emperor Adrian, wrote the life and times of the Emperors from Augustus to Domitian ; and if we except the doubtful allusion to them in the reign of Claudius, he does not even make use of the word Christian, or speak of anything in connection with them. During the time of which we have been speaking, lived and wrote Quintilian, Juvenal, Statius, and Martial.

## CHAPTER XVIII.

The office of Bishop foreign to churches established by
Paul, which were too poor and too few in number to
support the order.—Third chapter of the second
Epistle to Timothy, and the one to Titus, forgeries.
—The writings of the Fathers corrupted.

ELDERS or Seniors, in ancient Jewish polity,
were persons who were selected on account of
their *age* and *experience*, to administer justice
among the people,—who also held the first rank
in the synagogue as presidents. The office of the
Elder, with the Jews, commenced with Moses,
and was continued until after the days of the
Apostles. They were selected with reference to
age and knowledge, without regard to anything
else. It is evident that the Apostles did not depart from the Jewish form of church government,
but adopted and continued it during their lives.
The epistle of James was written in A.D. 61.
At that time the church was governed by Elders. " Is any sick among you ? let him call
for the Elders of the church ; and let them

pray over him, anointing him with oil in the name of the Lord." (*James* v. 14.)   In A.D. 64, Peter was an Elder, for that is the date of the first epistle which bears his name.   "The *Elders* which are among you I exhort, who *am also an Elder.*" (1 *Peter* vi. 1.)

We hear nothing of the office of Bishop until we enter the second age of Christianity, when the Therapeutæ had taken possession of the church, got the upper-hand of Paul and his followers, and introduced their government of the Episcopacy.   Did Paul institute a government for the churches established by him, different from that of Peter and James ?

Paul had no place for the office of Bishop in the churches which he founded and organized. In all cases except one he addresses his epistles to the church, and those that are sanctified in Christ.   The letter to the Romans is addressed, " To all that be in Rome, beloved of God." The first to the Corinthians, " Unto the church of God which is at Corinth ;" second Corinthians, " Unto the church of God which is at Corinth, with all the saints which are in all Achaia ;" Galatians, " And all the brethren which are with me, unto the churches of Galatia ; " Ephesians, " To the saints which are at Ephesus, and to the faithful in Christ Jesus ; " Thessalonians, " Unto the church of the Thessalonians, which is in God." Only in one instance does Paul make any other or different address. His epistle to the Philippians is addressed, " To all the saints in Christ Jesus which are at Philippi, *with the Bishops and Deacons:*" a simple spurious addition to the forms of address in all other cases.

The letter to the Philippians was written in A. D. 62 or A. D. 63, when Paul was in Rome. The epistle to the Thessalonians was written in A. D. 52, while he was in Corinth. For ten years Paul had been writing letters to the different churches, and in his epistle to the Philippians he uses the word Bishop for the first time. In this epistle the name of the Bishop is not given, which is significant. The contents of this letter show that there was no Bishop at Philippi at the time it was written.

When Paul was a prisoner in Rome the first time, the church at that place sent Epaphroditus to visit him, with means to supply his wants.

Thankful for the remembrance in which he was held, he sent the letter spoken of, and as some return for their kindness, he promised to send to them Timothy. " But I trust in the Lord Jesus to send Timotheus shortly unto you, that I also may be of good comfort, when I know your state." (*Phil.* ii. 19.) " Him therefore I hope to send presently, so soon as I shall see how it will go with me." (Chap. ii. 23.) If there was a Bishop in the church at Philippi, why not mention his name? or why send Timothy to them at all to supply their spiritual wants ?

How many members composed the church at Philippi to require the services of a Bishop and deacons ? Paul had been there once, and perhaps the second time. He was called there for the first time by a vision ; but he soon got into trouble, and even into prison, and remained but a short time. The author of the life of Paul (Renan) claims that he went into Macedonia the second time, and remained about six months, from June to November (page 261). The same writer says : " A country was reputed evangelized when the name of Jesus was pronounced there and half a score of persons had been converted. A church frequently contained no more than twelve or fifteen members. Probably all the converts of St. Paul in Asia Minor, Macedonia, and Greece did not exceed one thousand." Of this number, in a note to the twenty-second chapter, he assigns two hundred to the churches in Macedonia. As Paul had numerous churches in Macedonia, we are safe to assign to the church at Philippi the one-half of the whole number of his followers in that country. The first converts to Christianity were from the poorer class of people, and were not able to even support Paul, so that he had to maintain himself by manual labor as a tentmaker. The question may well be asked, what necessity was there for a Bishop and deacons at Philippi, and how were they to be supported?

Lucian, in his dialogue entitled Philopatris, while he no doubt exaggerates the poverty and mean appearance of Paul's followers, he at the same time throws much light on their true condition. He speaks of them as " a set of tatterdemalions, almost naked, with fierce looks." (Taylor's *Diegesis*, 376.) The truth is, all the churches which owe their origin to Paul were so small and so poor, that their government was of the most simple and economical kind. The first epistle of Paul to Timothy is intended to settle the position and claims of a Bishop in the church, and give the authority of Paul to the order. It is by such obvious forgeries as this, and others we will produce, that we are able to form any idea of the violence of the quarrels among the early Christians, as to the rights or standing of a Bishop in the church.

What arouses suspicion, and at last *convinces* us, that the third chapter of the first epistle to Timothy is a forgery, is that there is too much on the subject of Bishops from Paul all at once. If the episcopate form of government under-laid or was at the bottom of Paul's mode of government, it surely would have come to the surface or made itself known before it suddenly starts up in the first to Timothy; for he had been engaged in building up churches for at least fifteen years before that.

It is characteristic of the forgeries of the second century, when they are inserted into genuine writings, to make their appearance in

11*

the form of boulders, very much condensed, but out of place.   There is nothing diffusible about them, and we never suspect their presence until we stumble upon or over them.   The way the subject of Bishops is introduced, at once creates suspicion.   "This is a true saying.   If a man desire the office of a bishop, he desires a good thing."   It is intended to convey the idea in the start, that the office had been long in existence, and that the profits were such as to excite the cupidity of men.   The office of Bishop, in the time of Paul, even if such an office had any existence, was not, as we have shown, a good thing, but the opposite ; but in the second century, when the forgery was per- petrated, it was.   Good critics have pronounced the whole of the first of Timothy a forgery. The weight of the evidence is in favor of this belief.   As to the third chapter, there can be no question.

The effort to make it appear that Paul recog- nized the episcopate form of church government is repeated in the epistle to Titus.   It is to be remarked that this effort is only made in the last epistles written by him.   The first of Timothy was written in A. D. 64; that to Titus in A. D. 65. All the epistles between A. D. 52 and A. D. 62, have nothing to say on the subject of Bishops. Those written between these two periods, at Paul's death had obtained a wide circulation among all the churches of Asia and Europe, which made it impossible for those who were engaged in corrupting his writings to make changes that could be easily detected and exposed. As long as he lived it could not be done. But the reverse is true of those which were written just before his death. Besides, the Therapeutæ element did not begin to work until A. D. 57, and had not grown bold and strong enough to venture on the corruptions of Paul's writings until some time after his death.

The inference that is meant to be drawn from parts of his epistle is that Titus was a Bishop when Paul left him in Crete. Compared with other countries where Paul had churches, Crete was comparatively insignificant, and if Paul's converts in Europe and Asia did not exceed one thousand, and we have no reason to think they did, what portion of this number can we assign to the church at Crete, if there was one there at all? Renan says, "A church frequently contained no more than twelve or fifteen members." (*Life of Christ*, page 326.) Twelve or fifteen Christians and not more, if that many, composed the church at Crete. Did that number require the presence of a Bishop and elders?

The real truth of the matter is easily discovered. Paul, in A. D. 64, made a visit to all the churches in company with Titus and others, and stopped at Crete, which was the first time he was ever on the island, so far as we have any proof on the subject. After making some few converts, he left Titus to continue the work (*Titus* i. 5), while he proceeded west in the direction of Macedonia. The epistle to Titus was written from Nicopolis in the summer or fall of A. D. 64, and says: "For this cause left I thee in Crete, that thou shouldest set in order the things that are wanting, and ordain elders in every city, as I had appointed thee." (Chap. i. 5.) That is, to organize churches and appoint the elders.

Had this subject about church organization ceased at this point, there would not be much to complain of, although the word "*ordain*" had no place in the vocabulary of Paul. He ordained no one, after any form or ceremony, nor did he pretend to impart to his followers any but his own spirit and power.

In the seventh verse he proceeds to address Titus as Bishop, and to give him advice. Titus was no Bishop when Paul left him in Crete, nor did he hold any office, but was simply a fellow-laborer, like Luke, Mark, and Timothy. The men of the second century would have it understood that Paul was surrounded by a galaxy of Bishops. "For a bishop must be blameless, as the steward of God; not self-willed, not soon angry, not given to wine, no striker, not given to filthy lucre." (*Titus* i. 7.) Was it necessary to give such advice to "Titus, mine own son after the common faith?" The forgery is a clumsy one because it is out of place, and evidently inserted for a purpose. Titus was directed by Paul to leave Crete and meet him in Nicopolis, where he meant to spend the winter.

As has been stated, the only means we have of judging of the resistance made to the claims of the Bishop is from the extravagance of these demands, and the violence with which they are asserted. "Wherefore it becomes you to run together, according to the will of your Bishop, even as also ye do. For your renowned Presbyter, worthy of God, is fitted as exactly to the Bishop as the strings are to the harp." (*Ignatius to the Eph.*, sec. 4.) "Let no man deceive himself: Except a man be *within the altar* he is deprived of the bread of life." (*Ib.*, sec. 5.) "I exhort you, that you study to do all things in a divine concord, your Bishop presiding in *the place of God.*" (*Ignatius to Magnesians*, sec. 6.) "It is therefore necessary that you do nothing without your Bishop, even as ye are wont. In like manner, let all reverence the Deacons *as Jesus Christ*, and the *Bishops as the Father;* without these *there is no church.* Wherefore guard yourselves against such persons: And that ye will do, if ye are not puffed up, but continue inseparable from Jesus Christ our God; and from your Bishop and from the commands of the Apostles. He that is within the altar is pure. But he that is without, is not pure. That is, he that doeth anything without the Bishop and the Presbyters and Deacons is not pure in conscience." (*Ignatius to*

*Trallians,* secs. 2, 3, 7.) "But the Spirit spake, saying in this wise: Do nothing without the Bishop; But God forgives all that repent, if they return to the *unity of God* and to *the council of the bishop.*" (*Ignatius to Phil.*, sec. 8.) "See that ye all follow your Bishop as *Jesus Christ the Father.*" (*Ignatius to Smyrnæus,* sec. 8.) "It is good to have due regard both *to God and to the Bishop.*" (*Ib.*, sec. 9.)

These passages prove, that there was a party in the church that was opposed to the order of Bishops, introduced by the Therapeutæ, and that party no doubt were the followers of Paul. To silence them, the Epistles of Paul and the writings of the fathers were filled with forgeries and alterations so extravagant and obvious that they have defeated the object in view.

It is hardly necessary to ask the question, where it was the Therapeutæ form of government, by Bishops, was first organized. Alexandria seems to have been the common mother of all that is new in religion. It is here where have sprung up, in all ages, those subtle questions which have led the minds of men from sense and reason to pursue mischievous phantoms.   We infer from the writings of Eusebius, and from other sources, that the Therapeutæ Christians in Alexandria were numerous at an early date.   The letter of Adrian from Alexandria, in A. D. 134, is the first notice we have of a church with a Bishop at its head.   It was this letter that led the author of the "Decline and Fall," after a careful survey of the subject, with a penetration that nothing escaped, and an industry which left no ground unexplored, to conclude that the first regular Christian church government was instituted at Alexandria.   If Christian churches are not indebted to the Therapeutæ for their form of church government, from what source do they derive it ?   *Not* from the Jews ; not from Paul ; not from the Apostles.

# CHAPTER XIX.

Linus never Bishop of Rome.—Clement, third Bishop, and his successors to the time of Anicetus, myths.—Chronology of Eusebius exposed, also that of Irenæus.

AT what time was Linus, said to be the successor of Peter, made Bishop of Rome? The last trace we have of him, he was with Paul, in Rome, in the fall of A. D. 65. After this we know nothing of him, except from vague and more than doubtful tradition. According to Irenæus, it was when Peter and Paul were in Rome together, after they had laid the foundation of the church at that place. Paul went to Rome for the first time in A. D. 61, where he remained to the spring of A. D. 63. We have shown that during this time Peter was not there. Paul remained absent until the summer or fall of A. D. 65, and soon after his return was committed to prison. In A. D. 64, Peter was in Babylon, two thousand miles away. As Irenæus is the founder of the story, and the only authority in subsequent ages, when it was that Linus was appointed over the church of Rome as the successor of Peter, it devolves on those who pretend to believe him to show when it was that Peter and Paul were together in Rome, laying the foundation of a church, or anything else. This can never be done ; and if not, it destroys the first link in the Apostolic chain, and what is left is worthless.

The importance attached to Clement as the third Bishop of Rome will be a sufficient excuse for a critical examination, as to who he was, when he lived, and the position he occupied. The authority that Clement was Bishop of Rome is the same we have in any other case for links to keep up the Apostolic succession ; for Irenæus not only supplies an Apostle from whom to start, but also the intermediate links in the chain, to the time of authentic history. In this he finds great assistance in his ready invention of traditions, which we are required to believe without question, for fear of incurring the sin of unbelief, and subject ourselves to being called *slippery eels*, trying to evade the truth. The following is his language : " The blessed Apostles, then, having founded and built up the church, committed into the hands of Linus the office of the episcopate. Of this Linus, Paul makes mention in the epistles to Timothy. To him succeeded Anacletus ; and after him, in the third place from the Apostles, Clement was allotted the bishopric. This man, as he had seen the blessed Apostles, and had been conversant with them, might be said to have the preaching of the Apostles still echoing (in his ears), and their traditions before his eyes." (*Irenæus*, book iii. chap. 3, sec. 3.)

It may be affirmed with confidence, that we know nothing of the person who is called Clement, and made third Bishop in the Church of Rome. If he had held the office at the time it is claimed he did—the latter part of the first century—it would have been in the power of Irenæus to give us a full account of him : when he took the office, and when he died ; for if he had been a real character, there must have been persons living, at the time Irenæus flourished, who had seen and known him, so that the historian had ample material to inform posterity of everything which related to the life of the third Bishop.   But he gives no information—does not give a date—or the source from which he derives his authority, but has left the world to grope in darkness ever since.   We have his word, and that is all.

It is impossible that a person should fill an office of importance in the church in Rome, at the end of the first century, without leaving some tangible evidence that he had once an existence ; but Clement, like a shadow, passes over the earth, without a single mark of. any kind to prove he ever lived.   There is a dispute, as to when and how he died.   Some say he was banished into the Crimea by Trajan, and there suffered martyrdom by drowning.   Others that he died a peaceful death, A.D. 100.   There is nothing known about him, and for that reason, everything which concerns him is variously stated.   This could not be, had he been a real character in history.   It is only fictions of the brain that elude you, when you attempt to grasp them.

We are not told when he first filled the office which it is claimed he did.   Eusebius states, that he succeeded Anacletus in the twelfth year of Domitian's reign, A. D. 93. Cave, in his life of Clement, from the best light he could get, adopted the conclusion of Dodwell, that he became bishop about A. D. 64 or A. D. 65. The reason of this confusion is readily explained. The Clement referred to by Paul has been made to fill the place of an imaginary Clement at the end of the century—a person who only existed in the brain of Irenæus; and in trying to fix time and dates, the real and imaginary Clement create confusion. Irenæus has purposely left the subject in darkness, as he does the time when Peter went to Rome, and John to Asia. Dates are always fatal to falsehood and misrepresentations. The real Clement is referred to by Paul in the fourth chapter and third verse of the epistle to the Philippians, which was written from Rome in A. D. 63. This is the only notice that is taken of him, and he is made the third Bishop of Rome by Irenæus, simply because his name is found among others in one of Paul's epistles, as it was in the case of Linus, who was made first.

Who was it that wrote the letter to the Corinthians ascribed to Clement ?  We cannot tell who wrote all, but we can who did write a part. The address of this letter by a person who, it is claimed, was at the time a Bishop, to a church outside the city, which, it was said, appealed to him for advice, is the first bold attempt, on the part of the See of Rome, to enforce an acknowledgment of the supremacy of the Papal authority.  Can any reason be given why the church at Corinth, during the first century, should appeal to Rome for advice on any subject ?  The church at Corinth was the oldest, and after Paul's death knew of no higher authority than itself.  There are no signs of a church to which an appeal could be made to the end of the century, except those manufactured by the aid of tradition, which do not deserve to be mentioned when men mean to be serious.

This letter, like everything else suspicious, has no date.  We can fix the date with almost entire certainty to every letter written by Paul, and there is no reason why a date should not be given to the one to the Corinthians, except that there is something wrong about it, and a date would expose the fraud.  Archbishop Wake supposes it to have been written soon after the termination of the persecution under Nero, between the years A. D. 64 and A. D. 70. Lardner refers it to the year A. D. 96. (*Chevallier H. E. Introduction.*) The writer of this epistle was careful to leave no internal evidence by which its date could be determined, and what there is of that character is inserted apparently to mislead or afford grounds for dispute.

We have a right to demand the letter of the Corinthians to Clement, to which his is the answer ; for it is more probable that a letter received at Rome of so much importance would be preserved, than one sent away into a distant country. We not only have not the letter, but we cannot learn what it was about. There can be no doubt of the early date of the letter, for it makes no allusion to the Gospels, and was written during the lives of the first fathers of the church, such as Polycarp and Ignatius. It has but little of the odor of the second century about it.

From all the light we can collect on this perplexing question, we would say .that the letter itself was written by some of the early fathers, and made afterwards, with some alterations, to

conform to the purposes for which it was wanted—
that is, the entering wedge of Papal supremacy.
It is evident that Irenæus is attempting to
make the Clement of Paul take the place of a
creature of his own creation, and thus impose
upon the world, as he did in the case of John
and Mark.

In manipulating the letter he provided for
Peter in Rome and Paul in the Occident.   In
naming the successors to Clement, Irenæus says :
"To this Clement there succeeded Evaristus.
Alexander followed Evaristus ; then, sixth from
the Apostles, Sixtus w   appointed ; after him
Telesphorus, who was gloriously martyred ;  then
Hyginus ;  after him, Pius ;  then after him,
Anicetus.   Soter having succeeded Anicetus,
Eleutherus does now, in the twelfth place from
the Apostles, hold the inheritance of the episcopate.   In this order, and by this succession,
the ecclesiastical *tradition* from the Apostles,
and the preaching of the truth, have come down
to us.   And this is most abundant proof that
there is one and the same vivifying faith, which
has been preserved in the church from the
Apostles until now, and handed down *in truth*."

Including Linus and Anacletus, here are twelve *traditional* bishops in succession. Why traditional? For the reason that most of them, and all, except the three last, are not real or historical characters. Commencing with Nero, about the time when the tradition commences, and coming down to, and including Commodus, cotemporary with Eleutherus, there are thirteen emperors, one more than the number of Bishops in the same time, and history gives the time when each was born, when each became a ruler, when each ceased to reign, the manner of his death, and the qualities for which each was distinguished. It was an age of chronology, when dates of important events were as carefully preserved as in our own day; and yet Irenæus has failed to give a single date in connection with his twelve traditional Bishops. We do not even know there was such a tradition, except that he says so, and we are very certain that there was no church in Rome to preserve it, if there was.

This vagueness and uncertainty—where certainty, if the statements were true, could be easily attained, but easily exposed, if false—

12

must have been used with great effect, by the philosophers of the third century, against Christians, for it forced Eusebius to fix up dates for each of these traditional bishops. He makes each appear in order, like so many shadows, and he reminds us, as he goes through the roll, of the showman in a panorama, who explains each figure as it takes its place on the canvas. What Irenæus dared not do in the second, Eusebius dared do in the fourth century. On such subjects, his whole history proves, he had no scruples ; and he admits, indirectly, that he has related whatever might redound to the glory, and suppressed all that could tend to the disgrace of religion.

It will be noticed that he gives no authority for his dates, for the reason that he has none. Irenæus could find none in the second century. It is not probable Eusebius would be any better supplied in the fourth. It is evident he went to work and divided the whole time in which it is claimed the twelve Bishops lived, between them, so as to make each appear at a given time, marked by the accession of the emperors who reigned during the traditional era. We

will give his statements as he makes them himself :—

" After Vespasian had reigned *about* ten years,
he was succeeded by his son Titus ; in the second year of whose reign, Linus, Bishop of the
church at Rome, who had held the office *about*
twelve years, transferred it to Anacletus."
(*Ecc. Hist.*, book iii. chap. 13.)  "In the twelfth
year of the same reign, after Anacletus had
been Bishop of Rome twelve years, he was succeeded by Clement."  (*Ib.*, book iii. chap. 4.)
" In the third year of the above-mentioned
reign (Trajan's), Clement, Bishop of Rome,
committed the episcopal charge to Euaristus,
and departed this life, after superintending of
the divine word nine years."  (*Ib.*, book iii.
chap. 34.)  " *About* the twelfth year of the reign
of Trajan, Euaristus had completed the eighth
year as Bishop of Rome, and was succeeded in
his episcopal office by Alexander."  (*Ib.*, book
iv. chap. 1.)  "In the third year of the same
reign (Adrian's), Alexander, Bishop of Rome,
died, having completed the tenth year of his
ministration.  Xystus was his successor."  (*Ib.*,
book iv. chap. 4.)  "And Adrian being now in

the twelfth year of his reign, Xystus, who had now completed the tenth year of his episcopate, was succeeded by Telesphorus." (*Ib.*, book iv. chap. 5.) "The Emperor Adrian, having finished his mortal career after the twenty-first year of his reign, is succeeded by Antoninus, called Pius, in the government of the Romans. In the first year of this reign, and in the eleventh year of his episcopate, Telesphorus departed this life, and was succeeded in charge of the Roman church by Hyginus." (*Ib.*, book iv. chap. 10.) "Hyginus dying after the fourth year of his office, Pius received the episcopate." (*Ib.*, book iv. chap. 11.) "Pius dying at Rome in the fifteenth year of his episcopate, the church was governed by Anicetus." (*Ib.*, book iv. chap. 11.) "It was in the eighth year of the above-mentioned reign, to wit, that of Verus, that Anicetus, who held the episcopate of Rome for eleven years, was succeeded by Soter." (*Ib.*, book iv. chap. 19.) "Soter, Bishop of Rome, died after having held the episcopate eight years. He was succeeded by Eleutherus." (*Ib.*, book v. Introduction.) "In the tenth year of the reign of Commodus, Eleutherus, who had held the episcopate thirteen years, was succeeded by Victor." (*Ib.*, book v. chap. 22.)

We give a list of the emperors, and the time of accession of each to the government of the Empire, commencing with Vespasian, coming down to the time of Commodus :

| | | | |
|---|---|---|---|
| Vespasian | began to reign July 1st, A.D. | | 69 |
| Titus | " " June 24th, " | | 79 |
| Domitian | " " Sept. 13th, " | | 81 |
| Nerva | " " Sept. 18th, " | | 96 |
| Trajan | " " Jan. 27th, " | | 98 |
| Adrian | " " Aug. 10th, " | | 117 |
| Antoninus Pius | " " July 10th, " | | 138 |
| Antoninus Verus | " " March 7th, " | | 161 |
| Commodus | " " March 17th," | | 180 |

The following tabular statement shows the year in which each Bishop took the office, according to the statement of Eusebius, and the number of years which each held it :—

| | | | | |
|---|---|---|---|---|
| Linus, | A.D. 69, | held office | 12 years |
| Anacletus, | " 81, | " | 12 " |
| Clement, | " 91, | " | 9 " |
| Euaristus, | " 101, | " | 8 " |
| Alexander, | " 110, | " | 10 " |
| Xystus, | " 120, | " | 10 " |

Telesphorus,    A.D. 129,    held office   11 years
Hyginus,        "   138,         "           4  "
Pius,           "   142,         "          15  "
Anicetus,       "   157,         "          11  "
Soter,          "   169,         "           8  "
Eleutherius,    "   177,         "          13  "

From A.D. 69, when Linus became Bishop, to the tenth year of Commodus, when Victor succeeded Eleutherus, the true time is one hundred and twenty-one years. The time, taking the period assigned to each traditional Bishop, is one ·hundred and twenty-three years. In making a dead calculation under the circumstances, while we would not expect to find any gross mistakes, we would expect to discover enough to detect the true character of the work, for truth can never be so skilfully counterfeited, but that we can readily distinguish it from that which is false and spurious. The difference between the skilful counterfeit and the genuine bill is often slight, so much so that none but experts can detect it; but it is this difference which termines its character.

If the time occupied by the Bishops had fallen short two years, we might account for it on the principle of an interregnum ; but where the time is in excess, it is proof of a blunder or mistake, on the part of some one who is engaged in a dishonest employment.

Clement became Bishop in A.D. 91, and filled the office for nine years. This leaves his successor to take his place in A.D. 100, whereas he took it in A.D. 101, one year after the office was vacant. Euaristus took the office in A.D. 101, held it eight years, to A.D. 109 ; his successor took his place in A.D. 110, leaving a gap of one year. Telesphorus became Bishop in A.D. 129, and served eleven years, which would leave the office vacant in A.D. 140 ; but his successor takes it in A.D. 138, two years before the death of his predecessor. Anicetus took the office in A.D. 157, and served eleven years, to A.D. 168. His successor, Soter, took the office in the eighth year of Verus, which would be A.D. 169. Here is a clear gap of one year.

It was intended that the time assigned to the Bishops should correspond with the true historic period, and be 101 instead of 103 years. There are three years of vacancies, and a lap of two years in the case of Telesphorus and Hyginus.　If we deduct this lap, it will stand one hundred and one, the true time.

Eusebius meant well and intended no offence to chronology, but blundered, and in fixing twelve dates only makes four mistakes.　During a time when accuracy of dates is more important than at any other, there seems to have been less care exercised than in the same space of time in any period of history; and indeed, since the foundation of Rome, over seven hundred years before Christ, to the end of the empire, there has not been so many mistakes and contradictions, as to dates which relate to successive rulers, as during this period of one hundred and twenty-one years.　But such is the difference between true and genuine, and false and spurious history.

Of the twelve traditional Bishops of Irenæus, Telesphorus is selected for the honors of martyrdom.　No period in Roman history could have been selected more unlikely and improbable for the death of a Christian Bishop at Rome on account of his religion, than the reign of Antoninus Pius.　Not one drop of Christian blood was spilt in Rome during his reign of twenty-three years. Not only was there no blood spilt in Rome, but he forbade the persecution of Christians in the provinces by an express edict. A modern writer, speaking of him, says : " Open to conviction, uncorrupted by the vain and chimerical philosophy of the times, he was desirous of doing justice to all mankind. Asia *propria* was still the scene of vital Christianity and cruel persecution. These Christians applied to Antoninus, and complained of the many injuries they sustained from the people of the country. Earthquakes, it seems, had lately happened, and the pagans were much terrified, and ascribed them to the vengeance of Heaven against Christians." (Milner, *C. H.*, vol. I., page 100.)

Here follows the edict of the pious Emperor, addressed to the enemies of the Christians : " As to the earthquakes which have happened in past times, or lately, is it not proper to remind you of your own despondency when they happened, and to desire you to compare your spirit with theirs, and observe how serenely they confide in God ? You live in practical ignorance of the Supreme God himself—you harass and

12*

persecute to death those who worship him. Concerning these same men, some others of the provincials wrote to our divine Hadrian, to whom he returned answer, that they should not be molested unless they appeared to attempt something against the Roman government. Many also have signified to me concerning these men, to whom I have returned an answer agreeable to the maxims of my fathers. *But if any person will still persist in accusing the Christians merely as such, let the accused be acquitted, though he appear to be a Christian, and let the accused be punished.*" Set up at Ephesus in the common assembly of Asia.

Is it possible that Telesphorus was put to death in Rome under the mild and gentle reign of such a man ?

If the persons who are named by Irenæus as Bishops were real and not fictitious, how is it that there was not something done or said by some or all of them, so as to connect them with the events which transpired during their lives ? They lived, if they lived at all, during the most eventful period of Roman history. It was during the period of the civil war, when Rome was reduced to ashes—when the Jewish nation was almost destroyed by the legions of Titus, Jerusalem rendered a desert place, and the victorious armies of Trajan added Armenia, Mesopotamia, and Assyria to the Empire. During a period of seventy years, filled with the most exciting scenes and mighty events the world has ever known, we have at least nine Bishops in Rome, whose presence is no more felt in the history of the times, than so many men who were dead and quietly resting in their graves. They do not even cast their shadows on the earth.

The first person on the list of these traditional Bishops who steps forth into the light, so that we see something real and tangible, is Anicetus. Hegisippus says, " After coming to Rome, I made my stay with Anicetus, whose deacon was Eleutherus." Taking the foregoing data as correct, Anicetus held the office of Bishop about A. D. 157. If the statement of Hegisippus is true, which we are inclined to believe, not because he says so, but because it is probable, he is the first person who had ever seen and talked with any of the traditional Bishops of Irenæus, and he is tenth in order of succession. But it is not until we come to Eleutherus that we have a historic character, whose acts can be traced and found in the history of the times. Here we part company with spectres and deal with real life; but as we leave an age populated by phantoms, we enter into another stained with forgeries and fraud.

# CHAPTER XX.

The prophetic period.—The fourteenth verse of the seventh chapter of Isaiah explained.

THE claims of Christ to be the Logos or Son of God, in the Alexandrian sense, are made manifest by prophecy and miracles. The Jews, influenced by the prophets of their nation, believed that a deliverer would some day appear, who would deliver them out of the hands of all their enemies, and establish a temporal kingdom on the earth. But up to the time when Christ appeared, and even to the present day, no one had shown himself who realized their idea of this divine mission. The Christians at the time of Christ believed that he was the one spoken of by the old prophets, and that a spiritual deliverer, one who was to deliver men from the power of Satan, had been mistaken for one who with temporal power would rescue the Jewish people from the hands of their foes.

Barnabas, the companion of Paul, firmly believed this to be so, and took pains to cite many texts from the Old Testament to prove it. He cites numerous passages from Daniel, and all the prophets, and especially searched the pages of Isaiah, where he claims to have found at least sixteen different references made to Christ as the coming Saviour. But in all his references to the prophecies he makes none to the celebrated passage in the seventh chapter of Isaiah, on which is founded the doctrine of the divine conception of Christ from a Virgin. He makes no allusion to the fourteenth verse of the chapter at all, so that he was ignorant of the very foundation on which the Christianity of the second century was reared. Nor does Polycarp or Ignatius, except where their writings have been clearly defaced by the forgeries of men, who wished to establish the new ideas of the day by the authority of the fathers.

But when we come down to the second century, as far as the times of Justin Martyr, we find pages in the writings of the day filled with a new class of citations from the Old Testament, all of which foreshadow the appearance of Christ, his birth from a virgin, and point him out as the one foretold by the prophets. . In his Apology to the emperor, Justin Martyr quotes numerous passages from the Old and New Testaments to prove the divine mission of Christ, and speaks of his miraculous conception from the Virgin. (*Apology*, sec. 43.)

We now enter a new era, filled with new ideas, and passages of Scripture which before had been overlooked, but which all at once were discovered to contain a meaning which concerned the eternal interests of mankind. The Synoptics are now spread out before the world, and Christianity, armed by the voice of the prophets of God, is prepared to make a new start. One fact will appear clear as we approach the end of this subject, that all the men who undertook to strengthen the cause of Christianity by the application of prophecy to the person of Christ were ignorant of Jewish history, and either wofully misunderstood the language of the prophets, or foolishly attempted to pervert it.

There are four prophecies cited in the Gospel of Matthew from the Old Testament, which it is claimed point out Christ as the one foretold by the old Jewish prophets.  1st.  " Behold, a virgin shall be with child, and shall bring forth a son, and they shall call his name Emmanuel, which being interpreted is, God with us." (Matt. i. 23.)   It must be borne in mind, as has been before stated, that when the new idea of the Logos was started, it was found necessary in some way to make Christ more than mortal.  To be the Son of God in the Alexandrian sense he must have God for his father, and this could be only brought about through a virgin overshadowed by his divine presence.  In the zeal of these men, who undertook to prove it, they selected a passage from Isaiah which had no application to anything outside of the Jewish history of the day.

Rezin, king of Syria, and Pekah, king of Israel, united and made war on Ahaz, king of Judah, and marched upon Jerusalem.  Ahaz became alarmed at the combination, and feared the capture of the holy city and the destruction of his kingdom.  The Lord took compassion on him and his people, and sent Isaiah to him with an order to meet him at the end of the conduit of the upper pool, where he would inform him

what would be the fate of Judah and her enemies.

"Then said the Lord unto Isaiah, Go forth
now to meet Ahaz, thou, and Shear-jashub thy
son, at the end of the conduit of the upper pool
in the highway of the fuller's field ; and say unto
him, Take heed, and be quiet ; fear not, neither
be faint-hearted for the two tails of these smoking
firebrands, for the fierce anger of Rezin with Syria, and of the son of Remaliah.   Because Syria,
Ephraim, and the son of Remaliah, have taken
evil counsel against thee, saying, Let us go up
against Judah, and vex it, and let us make a
breach therein for us, and set a king in the midst
of it, even the son of Tabeal.   Thus saith the
Lord God, It shall not stand, neither shall it
come to pass.   For the head of Syria is Damascus, and the head of Damascus is Rezin : and
within threescore and five years shall Ephraim
be broken, that it be not a people.   And the
head of Ephraim is Samaria, and the head of
Samaria is Remaliah's son.   If ye will not believe, surely ye shall not be established.   Moreover, the Lord spake again unto Ahaz, saying,
Ask thee a sign of the Lord·thy God ; ask it

either in the depth, or in the height above.  But Ahaz said, I will not ask, neither will I tempt the Lord.   And he said, Hear ye now, O house of David ; Is it a small thing for you to weary men, but will ye weary my God also ?  Therefore the Lord himself shall give you a sign : behold, a virgin shall conceive, and bear a son, and shall call his name Immanuel.  Butter and honey shall he eat, that he may know to refuse the evil, and choose the good.  For before the child shall know to refuse the evil, and choose the good, the land that thou abhorrest shall be forsaken of both her kings.  The Lord shall bring upon thee, and upon thy people, and upon thy father's house, days that have not come, from the day that Ephraim departed from Judah ; even the king of Assyria."  (*Isaiah* vii. 3–17.)

The Lord told Ahaz not to fear or be faint-hearted, and he undertook to tell him how long it would be before Rezin and Pekah would be defeated and driven away.  In fixing the time, Isaiah indulges in a poetic license, and purposely rendered it obscure.  The language used expresses this meaning : If a virgin should conceive from that time, the day when the Lord spoke to Ahaz, the child would be born before his enemies would be subdued or driven away ; but not a great while before, for when they were driven away, the child would still be so young as not to know how to refuse the evil and choose the good. If the Lord did not tell Ahaz in some way when his enemies would be subdued, then the object of the interview entirely failed ; for that was just what Ahaz wanted to know, and which the Lord promised to disclose to him. Be not faint-hearted, neither be afraid, for in such a time your deliverance shall come. If the Lord wished to inform him that he would be delivered from Rezin and Pekah, after the Messiah spoken of in the Scriptures should come, which happened seven hundred years later, he would know no more *after*, than he did before he conversed with the Lord. The Lord did not tell him the precise day, but furnished Ahaz the data by which he might make his own calculations.

A very simple answer is purposely obscured by connecting some things with it which have a remote bearing on the subject, and others which have no connection with it at all. "Butter and honey shall he eat, that he may know to refuse the evil and choose the good," is an obscure allusion to the age of the child : and his name shall be called Immanuel, is of no significance, for he might as well be called by any other name. When we first read the passage, we see nothing distinct : all is in a kind of penumbra ; but after looking for a short time, as in a curiously shaded picture, an image, an idea, shows or appears on the ground-work, well marked and defined.

The explanation we have given of the passage from Isaiah is justified and made apparent by the language used in the first, second, and third verses of the eighth chapter of this prophet. It seems the Lord wished to prove to Ahaz, by actual demonstration, that what he promised should be fulfilled to the letter. The prophet says, he took with him two faithful witnesses and went in to the prophetess (who was the virgin) and she conceived and bare a son. Then when the son was born, the Lord said to the prophet, that before the child could pronounce the name of *father* or *mother*, "the riches of Damascus and the spoil of Samaria shall be taken away before the king of Assyria." Tiglath Pileser, king of the Assyrians, did come to the aid of Ahaz, and made war on the Syrians—laid their country waste—took Damascus, and slew Rezin. He afflicted the land of Israel, and carried the people away captives. (Josephus, *Antiq.*, book ix. chap. 12, sec. 3.) All this too within the time promised Ahaz, according to Isaiah.

The mystical language used by Isaiah in the fourteenth verse of the seventh chapter, which has been the cause of so much speculation and false interpretation, springs from the poetic element of the Hebrew mind. Had Isaiah lived in our day, his sublime genius would have produced a Paradise Lost ; but in his own country, and in his own times, his imagination dwelt upon ideas and thoughts which had their root in the hearts of the Jewish people. The Hebrew poets found subjects within the history of their own nation best suited to arouse their genius, and move the hearts of the people. The sorrows and afflictions brought on the nation by her enemies, and her final deliverance by the hand of the Lord, are favorite themes, and inspire her poets with thoughts full of tenderness, and with denunciations which are sublime and often terrific.  The harp of Zion in the hands of the daughters of Judah, as they weep by the waters of Babylon, gives forth no sounds but those of sorrow; but the genius of her prophets, inspired by a consciousness that a time of deliverance will come, deals out thunderbolts on the heads of their oppressors.

What are called the prophecies of Isaiah are nothing more, many of them, than so many epic poems, like the Iliad of Homer, to celebrate scenes and real occurrences in Jewish history.  The war upon Ahaz, king of Judah, by Rezin and Pekah, kings of Israel and Syria, took place during the life of Isaiah : and the poet undertakes to commemorate the history of the times, in the form of a Jewish epic.  He speaks of the past, and not of things to come.  The Jews were taught to believe that their nation was the favorite people of God, and from the time of Moses to the last of her prophets, her poets did not hesitate to introduce the Lord, and cause him to take part in a Jewish epic, any

more than Homer hesitated to introduce Jupiter
and all the heathen gods into the story of the
Iliad. The meeting of the Lord and Ahaz at
the "end of conduit of the upper field," and
what afterwards takes place, is the poetic license
of the poet, as he undertakes to narrate a portion of the history of his own time.

## CHAPTER XXI.

Bethlehem the birthplace of Christ, as foretold by the
prophets.—Cyrus, the deliverer and ruler referred to
by Micah the prophet.—The Lamentations of Jeremiah spoken of by Matthew (Chap. ii. 18), refers to
the Jews, and not to the massacre of the infants by
Herod.

WHEN Herod inquired of the wise men
where Christ should be born, they said unto
him, "In Bethlehem of Judea: for thus it is
written by the prophet, And thou Bethlehem,
in the land of Juda, art not the least among the
princes of Juda: for out of thee shall come a
Governor, that shall rule my people Israel."
(*Matt.* ii. 5, 6.)

The passage is taken from the prophet Micah,
who was a cotemporary with Jeremiah, and
prophesied under the reigns of Jotham, Ahaz,
and Hezekiah, kings of Judah.  He lived during
the time of Nebuchadnezzar, the great enemy
of the Jewish nation, and witnessed a large
share of the miseries he inflicted upon that

people. We would infer from the first verse of the fifth chapter, that his book was written at a time when the armies of the king of Babylon were encamped around the walls of Jerusalem.

"Now gather thyself in troops, O daughter of troops : *he hath laid siege against us ;* they shall smite the judge of Israel with a rod upon the cheek." Looking forward to the time when the Jewish people will be delivered from the power of Nebuchadnezzar and the Assyrian nation, and of their conquest by some other power, the prophet, aroused by a prophetic spirit, announces that the time is coming when Israel shall again be free: "But thou, Bethlehem Ephratah, though thou be little among the thousands of Judah, yet out of thee shall he come forth unto me that is to be ruler in Israel ; whose goings forth have been from of old, from everlasting. Therefore will he give them up, until the time that she which travaileth hath brought forth : then the remnant of his brethren shall return unto the children of Israel. And he shall stand and feed in the strength of the Lord, in the majesty of the name of the Lord

13

his God; and they shall abide; for now shall he be great unto the ends of the earth." (*Micah* v. 2, 3, 4.)

In the tenth verse of the fourth chapter, the captivity of the Jews, and their transportation to Babylon, is distinctly announced, and they are told that while in the hands of the Assyrians, they shall be as a woman in travail; but that, like her, they should in time be delivered from suffering. The third verse of the fifth chapter declares that God will not interfere in the mean time, and that they must wait for deliverance, and submit to their sufferings, as unavoidable as in the case of the woman; that at the appointed time a deliverer would come, who would save and bring back a remnant of the people, who shall grow powerful and "be great to the ends of the earth."

Now it is deliverance from Assyrian captivity that is referred to, and it is to violate the fitness of time, place, history, and the state of the Jews to apply it to anything else. Amidst the awful fate impending over the Jewish people, they wanted something to encourage and sustain them; and the prophet undertook to do so, by a promise, that in time their captivity should cease, and they be allowed to return to their own country.

But deliverance is to come from Bethlehem Ephratah—words which sufficiently indicate from what quarter the deliverer was to come; and to give a false direction the word Ephratah is omitted in the text in Matthew. Bethlehem in Judea is surely not intended, but the country watered by the river Euphrates. A little poetic license to create obscurity—a peculiarity of the Jewish prophets—does not at all render the meaning doubtful. Cyrus was king of all the country watered by the Euphrates; and the Assyrian empire ceased to exist when he restored the Jews to their own country. Cyrus was a ruler in Israel. He took the direction of their affairs, ordered the temple to be rebuilt, and directed how the means were to be provided to pay the expense. (Letter of Cyrus to Sisinnes and Sathrabouzanes. Josephus, *Antiq.*, book xi. chap. 1, sec. 3.) Cyrus is the ruler alluded to, and not Christ. The deliverer was to be at the head of a very ancient people—the Medes and Persians—who "have been from old—from everlasting?" When did Christ rule over Israel? Never.

That Jesus lived at Nazareth until he grew to be a young man could not be disputed, and no doubt the fact was stated in the Hebrew Gospel of Matthew. He might live there, but he must be born in Bethlehem, and some excuse must be had to get Mary there at the precise time when his birth took place. The device of the tax to take her there at the time is weak and puerile, and proves that those who got it up were neither wise nor learned. Matthew barely alludes to Bethlehem as the place of Christ's birth. "Now when Jesus was born in Bethlehem of Judea, in the days of Herod the king, behold, there came wise men from the east to Jerusalem." Luke is more specific. "And it came to pass in those days that there went out a decree from Cæsar Augustus, that all the world should be taxed." (*Luke* ii. 1.) "And all went to be taxed, every one into his own city. And Joseph also went up from Galilee, out of the city of Nazareth, into Judea, into the city of David, which is called Bethlehem (because he was of the house and lineage of David), to be taxed with Mary his espoused wife, being great with child." (*Luke* ii. 3, 4, 5.)

The Jews were taxed at the place where their property, real or personal, was at the time of taxing, and not where their ancestors happened to be born. A law or decree of the kind mentioned would involve a movement of almost the entire population of Judea, and for no reason, unless it was to give the people a chance to defraud the tax-gatherer by concealing their effects.

The Cyrēnius mentioned was sent out by Cæsar " to be a judge of that nation (the Jews) and take an account of their substance." (Josephus, *Antiq.*, book xviii. chap. 1, sec. 1.) It would not be necessary for Joseph to go to Bethlehem, seventy-five miles away, where he had nothing, to give an account of his substance, when all he had was in Nazareth. Besides, Judea was at this time under the government of Rome, and if there ever had been a law among the Jews requiring each one of them to go to his native city to be taxed, the Romans could not have any object in enforcing it. Admit that Joseph was required to go to Bethlehem because David was born there several hundred years before, to be taxed : why was it necessary for Mary to go with him ?   He was to give to the Roman officer " an account of his substance : " and did this require the presence of Mary ?

The writer of Luke fixes the time when this tax was to be levied.   It was when Cyrenius was Governor of Syria.   Now this Cyrenius, according to Josephus, was a Roman senator, who was sent to Judea " to take an account of the substance of the people," as a basis of taxation.   This was after Archelaus, the son of Herod, had been deposed, and ten years after the death of Herod.   Christ was ten years old when Cyrenius was made Governor, so that the journey of Joseph and Mary to Bethlehem was ten years before the decree to tax was made. The following are the words of Josephus : " Now Cyrenius, a Roman senator, and one who had gone through other magistracies and had passed through them till he had been Consul, and one who, on other accounts, was of great dignity, came at this time into Syria, with a few others sent by Cæsar, to be a judge of that nation, *and to take an account of their substance."* (Josephus, *Antiq.,* book xviii. chap. 1, sec. 1.)

Had the writer of Matthew known anything of Jewish history, he never would have made so gross a blunder, and saved the immense amount of labor that it has taken to explain away the effects of his ignorance. One explanation of this mistake is, that there were two assessments —one about the time Jesus was born, and the other ten years after. The first has been proven to be a forgery, and was never made. (Renan's *Life of Christ*, chap. 1. See note.)

" In Ramah was there a voice of lamentation and weeping and great mourning. Rachel weeping for her children and would not be comforted." This, it is claimed, referred to the cruelties of Herod, to escape from which Joseph and Christ were forced to fly into Egypt; so that his subsequent return to Nazareth would answer to the prophecy, which says, " *Behold, from Egypt I have called my Son.*" In the first place, the story of Herod's cruelties in the case of the infants is an invention, without the least claim to truth, and was a lame excuse, as we have just stated, to get Christ into Egypt.

" Then Herod, when he saw he was mocked

of the wise men, was exceeding wroth, and sent forth and slew all the children that were in Bethlehem and in all the coasts thereof, from two years old and under, according to the time which he had diligently inquired of the wise men." A very short time, not more than two or three days, elapsed after the birth of Christ, when Herod, not hearing from the wise men, gave the command for the wholesale murder of the infants. It was certainly giving Herod more credit for cruelty than was necessary, even on that occasion, for as Christ was only a few days old when the order was given, it was useless murder to include all under two years: ninety-five per cent. of the infants might as well have been spared as not.

It is a matter of surprise that Josephus, the Jewish historian, who suffers nothing deserving notice to escape his pen, has made no mention of a fact which, if true, would have filled Bethlehem and the country round about it with mourning. He could afford to make mention of the quarrels in Herod's family; but not one word to say about the wholesale slaughter of the infants. The story is so absurd, so easily exposed, and of no possible use, that it is omitted in Mark, Luke, and John.

But if the story is true, what has it to do with the troubles of Rachel?  The passage from Jeremiah refers to a time in the history of the Jews when Jerusalem was taken and held by the Assyrians, and a great number of that people had taken refuge in Egypt.  The Jews were undergoing great afflictions, and God, through Jeremiah, undertakes to console and comfort them.  The Lord, in plain language, says:  I know that there is great suffering in Ramah—much lamentation and bitter weeping.  Israel has lost many of her children, and she suffers great sorrow and grief.  "Thus saith the Lord: Refrain thy voice from weeping, for thy work shall be rewarded, saith the Lord;  and they shall come again from the land of the enemy." (*Jeremiah* xxxi. 15, 16.)  What has this to do with the cruelty of Herod?

We have stated that the massacre of the infants was an invention to form an excuse to get Jesus into Egypt; for his return from that country would serve to prove that he was the one referred to when the Lord is made to say, " Out

13*

of Egypt I have called my son." Here, we confess, we are at a loss to express our astonishment. In the eleventh chapter of Hosea, the Lord complains of the ingratitude of the Jewish nation, and reminds them what he had done for them in times past. He expresses the love he had for them when the nation was young, and required the power of his arm to protect them. "*When Israel was a child, then I loved him, and called my son out of Egypt.*" (*Hosea* xi. 1.) It need not be said, that this refers to the deliverance of the Jews from the hands of Pharaoh. Israel is the son spoken of who had *already* passed out of Egypt. "And he came and dwelt in a city called Nazareth, that it might be fulfilled which was spoken by the prophets, *He shall be called a Nazarene.*" (*Matthew* ii. 23.) There is no such prophecy to be found in the Old Testament.

# CHAPTER XXII.

### Christ and John the Baptist.

" THE beginning of the gospel of Jesus Christ, the Son of God ; As it is written in the prophets, Behold, I send my messenger before thy face, which shall prepare thy way before thee. The voice of one crying in the wilderness, Prepare ye the way of the Lord, make his paths straight." (*Mark* i. 1, 2, 3.) As in Matthew, at the very outset, the second Gospel starts out to show that Christ is the one foretold by the prophets, and that a direct reference is made to him by Isaiah, as one who was to be preceded by another who was to prepare the way for his advent. Cotemporaneous history, and a critical examination of the words of the prophet, will dispel the delusion.

Hezekiah, king of Judea, was improvident enough to show to the son of the king of Babylon, then on a visit to him, all his treasures, and riches of every description; and "there was nothing in his house, nor in all his dominion, that Hezekiah shewed him not." When Isaiah was told by the king himself what he had done, the prophet spoke and said: "Hear the word of the Lord of hosts: Behold, the days come, that all that is in thine house, and that which thy fathers have laid up in store until this day, shall be carried to Babylon: nothing shall be left, saith the Lord. And of thy sons that shall issue from thee, which thou shalt beget, shall they take away; and they shall be eunuchs in the palace of the king of Babylon. Then said Hezekiah to Isaiah, Good is the word of the Lord which thou hast spoken. He said moreover, For there shall be peace and truth in my days." (*Isaiah* xxxix. 5, 6, 7, 8.) The Babylonian captivity is here referred to.

Isaiah then proceeds to declare that after great suffering, in their servitude under the Assyrians, the Lord would deliver the Jewish people, and that they should again be a great and prosperous nation. "Comfort ye, comfort ye my people, saith your God. Speak ye comfortably to Jerusalem, and cry unto her, that her warfare is accomplished, that her iniquity is pardoned : for she hath received of the Lord's hand double for all her sins. The voice of him that crieth in the wilderness, Prepare ye the way of the Lord, make straight in the desert a highway for our God. Every valley shall be exalted, and every mountain and hill shall be made low : and the crooked shall be made straight, and the rough places plain." (*Isaiah* xl. 1, 2, 3, 4.)

With what tenderness the prophet speaks to his countrymen, to assure them that their captivity will not last forever ! Divested of poetical language and figures, the Lord says : In your lost condition in slavery (" wilderness ") you shall hear the voice of the Lord to comfort you. Be prepared, for he will provide the means (" highway ") for your deliverance from captivity. The words wilderness, desert, and highway are symbolical terms, representing the lost condition of the Jews and the promise made by the Lord, that he would provide means for their deliverance from their enemies. What follows, holds forth to the Jews a glorious future. " Every valley shall be exalted, and every mountain and hill shall be made low." That is, the down-trodden and oppressed children of Israel shall once more take the stand of an independent nation ; and the proud and lofty Assyrian shall in his turn be humbled, and come under the yoke of the conqueror. The idea which underlies the language of the prophet is, that the Jews will be ultimately restored to their own country, and again become a prosperous people ; and as is characteristic of all these Jewish prophecies, the expressions, " and the crooked shall be made straight, and the rough places plain," are mere expletives, to obscure the sense, and increase the ambiguity. Like the oracles of Greece, a simple idea is concealed beneath figures and metaphors, and the mind distracted by the introduction of thoughts that have no meaning, and no connection with the subject.

Josephus, after giving a full account of this prophecy from Isaiah says, it was subsequently fulfilled in the captivity and restoration of the Jews, and that when he wrote, the words of the prophet had passed into history. (*Antiq.*, book x. chap. 2, sec. 2.) The Lord, by the prophet, is addressing the Jews of that day about matters which directly concerned them, and what was said had no more to do with John the Baptist preaching on the Jordan, in the neighborhood of the Arabian desert, than it had with the travels of Livingstone over the sands of Africa. The John referred to in Mark is a historic character, and all we know about him we learn through Josephus.

In his day he was a reformer. Shocked at the low condition of the Jews, who had reached the lowest deep in crimes and vices of all kinds, through the corruption of the priesthood, and tyranny of their civil Governors, he undertook to reform abuses, and elevate the moral standard of the nation. Standing on the banks of the Jordan, crowds from the surrounding country came to hear him denounce the sins of the people, and be baptized. He preached repentance, and those who did repent he purified with the mystic waters of the Jordan.

In the time of John, the Jewish people had become restive, and chafed under the government of Rome. The elements of rebellion were then at work, which, a few years later, led to open revolt, and the total ruin of the nation. While the Jews overran with discontent, the Roman Governors were filled with suspicion. Herod took alarm at the course of John, and caused him to be seized and confined in the castle of Macherus, situated on the borders of the desert, where he was afterwards put to death.   All that is known of him is found in the following extract from Josephus :

" Now, some of the Jews thought that the destruction of Herod's army came from God, and that very justly, as a punishment of what he did against John, that was called the *Baptist;* for Herod slew him, who was a good man, and commanded the Jews to exercise virtue, both as to righteousness towards one another, and piety towards God, and so to come to baptism ; for that washing [with water] would be acceptable to him if they made use of it, not in order to the putting away [or remission] of some sins [only], but for the purification of the body ; supposing still that the soul was thoroughly purified beforehand by righteousness. Now, when [many] others came in crowds about him, for they were greatly moved [or pleased]

by hearing his words, Herod, who feared lest
the great influence John had over the people
might put it into his power and inclination to
raise a rebellion (for they seemed ready to do
anything he should advise), thought it best, by
putting him to death, to prevent any mischief
he might cause, and not bring himself into difficulties, by sparing a man who might make him
repent of it when it should be too late.   Accordingly he was sent a prisoner, out of Herod's
suspicious temper, to Macherus, the castle I
before mentioned, and was there put to death.
Now the Jews had an opinion that the destruction of this army was sent as a punishment upon
Herod, and a mark of God's displeasure against
him."   (Josephus, *Antiq.*, book xviii. chap. 5,
sec. 2.)

It was this passage, and the one from Isaiah,
" The voice of him that crieth in the wilderness,
Prepare ye the way of the Lord," that suggested
the story of Christ coming from Galilee to the
Jordan to be baptized by John, and the scenes
that followed.   As Josephus, in the passage just
quoted, speaks of what John was doing on the
Jordan, and what occurred there, it is strange

he takes no notice of the wonderful things which took place at the time Christ was baptized, as described in Matthew. But, as we have shown, the prophecy of Isaiah has nothing to do with John the Baptist.

The story that the life of John was the price paid for a jig danced before Herod, is not only false and absurd, but in one sense impossible. Herod was a Roman officer, and received his appointment from Rome. As the Governor of a province, he acted under, and was governed by law. To take life without sufficient cause, from mere wantonness or caprice, subjected him to punishment and removal from office. Herod might put John to death as a promoter of sedition, but not to gratify the spite of a woman who had been accused of incest. Pilate dared not deliver over Christ to be crucified, until after he was charged by the Jews with conspiring against the government of Cæsar. His claim to be king of the Jews, which was made a charge against him, was the warrant which Pilate had to surrender him to a merciless mob, which would not be satisfied with anything less than his blood. The author of

Matthew, it is clear, was ignorant of the topography of Judea, the history of the Jews, and knew nothing of the fundamental principles of the Roman law.

# CHAPTER XXIII.

The miracle of the cloven tongues.—Misapplication of
a prophecy of Joel.

IN the Acts of the Apostles, a passage from
Joel the prophet is spoken of by Peter, as fore-
telling what is called the miracle of tongues.
At the end of forty days Christ appeared to his
disciples at Jerusalem, and being assembled together with them, they were commanded not to
depart from Jerusalem until certain things should
take place.　Now the writer of the Acts forgot
what he said in his Gospel, if he wrote both,
for he there tells us that Christ ascended the
day of his resurrection, or at most, the day after.
Taking what we can glean from the four Gospels, and taking the probabilities of the case
into the account, the disciples, a very short
time after the death of Jesus, returned to Galilee.　The public mind was greatly moved
against Jesus, which was more or less directed

against his followers, and as none of them were remarkable for courage, it is hardly probable that they would tarry in Jerusalem, especially as there was nothing to keep them.   But according to the writer in Luke, at the end of the forty days they were still in the city, and were commanded not to leave until certain things took place.

He next says, " And when the day of Pentecost was fully come, they were all with one accord in one place.   And suddenly there came a sound from heaven, as of a rushing mighty wind, and it filled all the house where they were sitting.   And there appeared unto them cloven tongues like as of fire, and it sat upon each of them.   And they were filled with the Holy Ghost, and began to speak with other tongues, as the Spirit gave them utterance." (*Acts* ii. 1, 2, 3, 4.)

This is something truly wonderful, and we are astonished that so strange and important an event has found no place in history—especially as a report of it must have been circulated far and wide, for the writer says, that " there were dwelling at Jerusalem, Jews out of every nation under heaven," who came to see for themselves. The writer includes other people besides Jews from every nation, and says : "Now when this was noised abroad, the multitude came together, and were confounded ;" and among these were "Parthians, Medes, Elamites, and the dwellers in Mesopotamia, and in Judea, and Cappadocia"—people from "Phrygia, Pamphylia, Cretans and Arabians"—and all heard spoken the language of their native countries.

Josephus lived not long after this time, and if he did not reside in Jerusalem, he must have been often in the Jewish capital, and if anything so wonderful as this had taken place, he certainly must have heard of it, and it was not possible for him to forget it when he came to write his history, especially as things of no comparative importance are fully noted by him.

These things are so wonderful, that it is necessary to explain them by the direct action of the Deity, in fulfilment of prophecy. The writer has Peter make a speech, and Peter tells the crowd that they need not be surprised, for what had just happened had all been foretold, and was nothing more than the fulfilment of a prophecy of Joel, who said: "And it shall come to pass in the last days, saith God, I will pour out my Spirit upon all flesh: and your sons and your daughters shall prophesy, and your young men shall see visions, and your old men shall dream dreams. And on my servants and on my handmaids I will pour out in those days of my Spirit; and they shall prophesy: and I will shew wonders in heaven above, and signs in the earth beneath; blood, and fire, and vapor of smoke: the sun shall be turned into darkness, and the moon into blood, before that great and notable day of the Lord come." (*Acts* ii. 17, 18, 19, 20.)

All this has nothing more to do with, or has no more reference to, the miracle of the cloven tongues than it has to the assassination of Julius Cæsar in the Roman Senate. The Jews, at the time referred to by Joel, were suffering under great afflictions. There had been a most severe drought, and the land had been devoured by the locust, the canker-worms and caterpillar. As all calamities which befell the Jewish people were referred by them to the displeasure of God on account of their sins, Joel exhorts them to repent, and promises, if they do, the Lord will come to the rescue. " Then will the Lord be zealous for his land and pity the people. He will send down rain, and the floors shall be full of wheat, and the vats shall overflow with wine and oil. And I will restore to you the years that the locust had eaten, the canker-worm and caterpillar and palmer-worm, my great army which I sent among you. And you shall eat in plenty and be satisfied, and praise the name of the Lord your God, that hath dealt wondrously with you. And ye shall know that I am in the midst of Israel, and that I am the Lord your God, and none else : and my people shall never be ashamed."

Now follows what Peter was made to say was the prophecy which foretold the miracle of the cloven tongues. " And it shall come to pass afterwards that I will pour out my Spirit on all flesh ; and your sons and your daughters shall prophesy, your old men shall dream dreams, and your young men shall see visions." Which means, I will pour out my blessings (" Spirit ") on all flesh, including the servants and hand-maids—they shall be universal, and not confined to any class. . Then all the young and the old shall rejoice and be happy. Their happiness shall be of the most exalted kind, unalloyed with care, like delightful dreams and visions. As the prophet had said in the beginning of this chapter : " Blow ye the trumpet in Zion, and sound an alarm in my holy mountain : let all the inhabitants of the land tremble : for the day of the Lord cometh, for it is nigh at hand ; a day of darkness and of gloominess, a day of clouds and of thick darkness, as the morning spread upon the mountains : a great people and a strong ; there hath not been ever the like, neither shall be any more after it, even to the years of many generations." (*Joel* ii. 1, 2.)

Referring to this terrible calamity which was to come, that the fear of it *might not interrupt this general state of happiness* which is spoken of, the Lord tells the people that he will give them timely notice, that they may be prepared : " And I will shew wonders in the heavens and in the earth, blood, and fire, and pillars of smoke. The sun shall be turned into darkness, and the moon into blood, before the great and the terrible day of the Lord come."

14*

(*Joel* ii. 30, 31.) There could not be a state of universal joy among the people, such as is described, as long as the "great and terrible day of the Lord" might overtake them any moment. There could be no happiness where there was constant fear. The Lord promised that a timely warning should be given. Now what has this beautiful and sublime poem to do with the miracle of the cloven tongues ?

## CHAPTER XXIV.

### Miracles.

IT is in vain to deny the truth of a miracle on the ground that it is impossible, and contravenes the well-established laws of the universe. The power to create, implies the power to suspend ; and as the performance of a miracle is the exercise of creative energy, it is just as easy to exercise it in one case as another. All efforts to demonstrate the impossibility of miracles have failed even in the hands of such men as Hume, because men reason on such subjects in a circle. Still it would be strange if there was no way to expose a false miracle, especially where the results claimed from it are calculated to lead men into error. When some unusual and extraordinary event which amounts to a miracle is said to have occurred one hundred years ago, at a time when intelligent and inquisitive minds were around, and no notice is taken of it by them in giving an account of their

own times, nor by any one else, it is safe to conclude that it never did take place, and that
those who assert it for the first time at the end
of the hundred years are engaged in an attempt
to impose some fraud on their fellow-men.

From the death of Christ, A.D. 33, to some
time near A.D. 140, we claim that no writer of
profane or church history makes mention or
speaks of the miracles described in the three
first Gospels, and not those of the fourth until
long afterwards. It is by negative testimony
alone that we can arrive at the truth. In the
first place, did the great Apostle of the Gentiles perform the miracles that are ascribed to
him in the Acts? It is stated that at Lystra he
cured a man who had been crippled from his
birth by his simple word; he exorcised the
evil spirit that was in Lydia; he raised Euty-
chus, who had fallen from a window; cast
from his hand, unhurt, the deadly viper; and
such miraculous powers did he possess, "that
from his body were brought unto the sick
handkerchiefs or aprons, and the diseases departed from them, and the evil spirits went out
of them." (*Acts* xix. 12.)

Paul, in his epistles, does not mention or refer to any of these wonderful things, and does any man suppose, if true, he would fail to make some allusion to them? He neither mentions the miracles ascribed to himself, nor those described in the four Gospels. Perhaps he did not disbelieve in the possibility of miracles, for such belief was common to the age; but to believe them possible, and believe that one has been performed, is another thing. "Truly the signs of an Apostle were wrought among you in all patience, in signs and wonders, and mighty deeds." (2 *Cor.* xii. 12.) The signs and wonders here spoken of were made to appear to the Corinthians alone, and have no reference to miracles described in the New Testament, nor do we know what they were, for no notice of them is taken in the Acts. In the 18th chapter and 9th verse, he says that he had a vision which told him not to be afraid to speak, and not hold his peace. The "mighty deeds" refers to his works as an Apostle, and the "signs and wonders," rather to the fruits of his preaching than to any display of miraculous power.

Had Paul possessed the power attributed to him in the Acts, it would have been easier for him to have converted the world than to make the few converts he made after the labor of a life. There were those living who in the course of nature might have seen Lazarus, or heard of his resurrection, and had it been in the power of Paul to have cited his case, or any of the miraculous cures claimed for Christ or any of his disciples, the conversion of mankind would have been as rapid as the movements of the earth. Every pagan temple and altar would have been deserted, and their priests have fallen prostrate at the feet of Paul. A few pretended miracles and revelations on the part of Mahomet established his claim to be the prophet of God, and were the means, backed by the scimitar, of fixing the faith of millions. Paul is silent on the subject of the miracles. Barnabas was a companion and fellow-preacher with Paul.

No document extant to-day which relates to the Apostolic age is entitled to more, if as much confidence and credit as the epistle which bears his name. For some reason, it bears less evidence on its face of fraudulent manipulation than any other writing of that time, and it is this evidence of its purity which excludes it from the list of canonical Gospels this day. It has been referred to by a long list of fathers, commencing with Origen, and coming down to writers of our day, as the genuine production of the companion of the great Apostle. No one, not even the Apostles themselves, had more faith in Christ than he, and it seems to be the burden of his epistle to prove that he was the Saviour who had been foretold by the prophets, and whom the Jews were anxiously expecting. Had Christ, in his ministry among men, done or performed any act out of the course of nature which proved him superior to other men in his power over the laws of nature—anything like command over diseases, sickness, to say nothing of death—Barnabas would not have failed to dwell upon everything of the kind with energy and zeal, because such powers would establish what he aimed to prove : that is, that Christ was the one spoken of by the prophets. But, while he makes the most labored application of the prophecies to Christ, he makes no allusion to any wonderful work he performed while he was on the earth.  He has not one word to say on the subject of the miracles ascribed to Christ in the Gospels.

Much may be inferred from the silence of Apollos on the subject of miracles.  The intercourse between the Jews at Alexandria and Judea was constant.  Nothing of importance could occur in Jerusalem without its being known in a short time on the banks of the Nile.  The history of John the Baptist, the works he did at the Jordan, and the manner of his death, were all known to Apollos from some source, before Josephus wrote his history of the Jews; but it seems he had never heard of Christ or any of his wonderful works.  (*Acts* xviii.)  After his conversion he taught that Christ was the one expected by the Jews, and he undertook to prove it by the prophecies in the Old Testament.  It would have been far easier to establish this by the mention of the one-half the miracles ascribed to Christ in the Gospels than by arguments drawn from prophecy, which were vague, obscure, and doubtful.  But he had never heard of the resurrection of Lazarus, nor of the miracles of the loaves and fishes, nor of the wonderful things that happened to the swine in the country of the Gadarenes.

There are now extant, writings which learned men refer to the Apostolic age, which have no value except as they may throw some light on the age in which they were written. We may mention the epistle of Paul to the Laodiceans; the epistles of Paul to Seneca, with Seneca's to Paul, and the Acts Paul and Thecla. In none of these writings is any mention made of the miracles of Paul, or those of the New Testament, and the silence of such works is only of consequence as it shows the universal ignorance of antiquity, or the Apostolic age, on the subject; for it is not to be supposed that those things which were standing themes for discourses and books in the second century, would be unnoticed in the first, if they did exist, as well at one time as the other. How can we account for the silence of the fathers of the church on this subject? Ignatius and Polycarp were so near to the time of Paul and the disciples, and even Christ, that nothing which concerned any one of them was unknown, and if the miracles ascribed to them had been real

14*

occurrences, nothing could be more effective in the hands of these fathers for the spread of the religion of Christianity.

But there is not only no mention by any one of them of the miracles, but the Gospels have not yet appeared.   Up to the beginning of the first century, there is no mention or reference made in any writing, either to the Gospels, or the miracles they describe.   Allusions are made in some cases to the Scriptures, in the most general terms; and as the Old Testament writings were called Scriptures, and there was the Hebrew Gospel of Matthew, and the epistles of Barnabas, James, Peter, and Paul, to which the term Scripture might apply, the reference is of no value in fixing the date of the Gospels.   The first distinct and unequivocal notice of the three first Gospels is found in Justin Martyr's *Apology ;* and he, who speaks of them for the first time, dilates on their contents, and refers to Matthew, Mark, and Luke each by name: to Matthew nineteen, to Mark four, and to Luke fourteen times.   From this time to the present hour, every book abounds in references to these Gospels.

As yet the Gospel of John had not appeared. What is remarkable in the Gospels, referred to by Justin, who makes a most elaborate disquisition on the prophecies, citing many passages to prove that Christ was a divine person, whose advent had been predicted, he does not make mention of any of his miracles, or of those of any of his disciples. He speaks of Christ's birth from the Virgin Mary, his miraculous conception, and all the leading acts of his life, as described in Matthew and others, but seems to have had no knowledge of the miraculous works he performed.

The silence of Justin on the subject of miracles, and his extended notice of the prophecies, can only be explained by the fact that there was nothing said about them in the Gospels, and that they were inserted at a later day. As the quarrels among Christians in the second century intensified, and as the authority of the church grew to be paramount as we approach the dark ages, no doubt the Gospels underwent a revision, and the miracles were added as a means to excite the awe and command the belief of the Pagan world. The spirit for the creation of miracles commenced in the church before the end of the second century—was encouraged by it, and has been continued down to our own times, and formed the most effective weapon for the conversion of the hordes of the North, and for the final overthrow of the followers of Arius. Each age had its own miracles, in each of which was apportioned the amount of divine energy required to subdue the obstinacy and unbelief to be overcome.

The silence of what are called profane writers on the subject of the miracles is equally unaccountable—if they are to be regarded as real occurrences in history—and none as much so as that of the Jewish historian, Josephus. Of sacerdotal extraction, and of royal descent, Flavius Josephus was born A.D. 37. He was alive in A.D. 96, but the time and manner of his death is unknown. His works comprise a complete history of the Jews, and omit nothing that was worthy of notice. He was a youth of great ability and promise, and says of himself, "When I was a child, and about fourteen years of age, I was commended by all for the love I had for learning, on which account the high priest and principal men of the city came frequently to me together, in order to know my opinion about the accurate understanding of points of law." (*Life of Josephus*, sec. 1.)

Here we have a historian of the right kind, living so near the time that he must have seen and conversed with those who had seen and known Christ and his disciples. How are we to regard his silence? Had Christ been the character which many suppose he was, a teacher endowed beyond all other men, with a divine genius to declare the doctrines which are to govern man in his relations towards the Creator and towards each other, we can well understand why, in A.D. 93, when Josephus wrote the history of the Jews, he failed to notice him. His ministry extended through a period of only three years, at a time when the Jewish people were chafing under the yoke of the Romans, and were preparing for a final struggle with the conquerors. At such a time, the presence of such a person as Christ, who taught men to forgive their enemies, to love their neighbors as themselves, and to cultivate feelings which dispose mankind to peace and charity, would most likely pass unnoticed. If Christ was more than a great teacher—if he were the second person in the Godhead, who condescended to visit the earth to instruct mankind, and while here performed the wonderful works spoken of in the Gospels, then there is no way in which we can account for the silence of the Jewish historian. We are forced to admit that the Son of God, who took up his abode among men to convince and instruct them, failed to make his presence known and felt so as to attract the notice of him who undertook to give a minute account of what happened at the time, and in the country where he preached and taught.

The attempt in the fourth century to force into history, between the regular course of events, a passage intended to break the force of total unconsciousness on the part of Josephus, that there was such a person as Christ, to the eye of the critic is infinitely more damaging than complete silence. A quarrel, which led to a sedition, sprang up in Jerusalem, about the use made by Pilate of sacred money, to bring water into the city. *" About the same time, also, another* sad calamity happened, which put the Jews into disorder." A Roman woman called Paulina, through the connivance of some of the gods of Isis, was seduced by a person of the name of Mundus. (*Antiq.*, book xviii. chap. 3.) Between these two events, is wedged, or forced in, a paragraph which contains all the great historian has to say of Christ, and the events of his life. Twenty-nine lines are taken to tell about the troubles growing out of the misapplication of the sacred money; one hundred and thirty-one about Paulina and her misfortunes, and *sixteen* are all that the historian requires to inform us of all he knows about Christ. Much better had he said nothing.

If Josephus makes no mention of Christ and his miracles, where must we look? It is in vain to search among the writers of Greece and Rome. Out of the nine reasons given by Dr. Lardner for believing the passage from Josephus in relation to Christ spurious, the first is sufficient: it was never quoted, or referred to, by any writer previous to *Eusebius*, who wrote in the fourth century.

## CHAPTER XXV.

### Epistle of Paul to the Hebrews.

THIS epistle has been the source of more controversy than any other book of the New Testament. It has been the cause of much useless labor and unprofitable research. In the first place, was Paul the author? Tertullian ascribes it to Barnabas; Grotius to St. Luke, and Luther the reformer thought it was written by Apollos, mentioned in the Acts; but the testimony of ecclesiastical antiquity is all in favor of Paul as the author. Allusions are made to it in the epistles of Ignatius about A. D. 107. It is also referred to by Polycarp, Bishop of Smyrna in the year A. D. 108.

Internal evidence, supplied by the epistle itself, is conclusive that Paul was the writer. No one better than he understood the veneration in which the Levitical law was held by the Jewish people, and the tenacity with which they adhered to it. As he believed that this law had passed away, and that the Lord had made a new covenant with the Jewish nation, it was natural for him to labor to open the eyes of his countrymen, and bring them under the light of the new dispensation. It was for this reason, when he entered into a place for the first time, that he always began to teach in the synagogue. If Paul wrote to the Hebrews at all, it would be just such an epistle as the one ascribed to him, except certain portions, which were clearly written after the Pauline period of Christianity had passed away.

Again, it has been a question as to the language in which this epistle was first written. At the time of Paul, the original Hebrew was understood by few, and had ceased to be the language of the Jews. The original Hebrew was broken in upon by several dialects—such as the East Aramæan, or Chaldee, and the West Aramæan, or Syriac. The universal language of the day was Greek, and no doubt Paul adopted it in writing to the Hebrews, who were dispersed over Europe, Asia, and parts of Africa.

As the initiatory formula usual in the epistles of Paul is wanting in this, it has been questioned whether it was really an epistle, or only a discourse intended for the general reader. The want of the usual formula can be easily account-ed for, when the mind becomes convinced that the first chapter is not the production of Paul. That it was written as it now stands by the for-gers of the second century admits of no doubt. The design of the writer is exposed in the very first and second verses of the first chapter. " God, who at sundry times and in divers man-ners spake in time past unto the fathers by the prophets, hath in these last days spoken unto us by his Son, whom he hath appointed heir of all things, *by whom also he made the worlds.*"

Here Christ is made the Creator by whom the worlds were made. Again: " Who being the brightness of his glory, and the *express image* of *his person*, and *upholding all things by the word of his power*, when he had by himself purged our sins, sat down on the right hand of the Majesty on high ; being made so much *bet-ter than the angels*, as he hath by *inheritance* obtained a more excellent name than they. For unto which of the angels said he at any time, Thou art my Son, this day have I begotten thee? And again, I will be to him a Father, and he shall be to me a Son? And again, when he bringeth in the first-begotten into the world, he saith, And let all the angels of God worship him." (*Heb.* i. 3–6.)

Here we find condensed into a few verses, and declared in the most pointed language, the *Godship* of Christ, first proclaimed by the men of the second century, and which is in direct conflict with the remainder of the Epistle, and with what Paul taught during his whole life.

Commencing at the ninth verse of the second chapter, Paul says: "But we see Jesus, who was made a little *lower* than the angels for the suffering of death, crowned with glory and honor; that he by the grace of God should taste death for every man." "For verily he took not on him the nature of angels; but he took on him the seed of Abraham." (Chap. ii. 16.) "Wherefore, holy brethren, partakers of the heavenly calling, consider the Apostle and *High Priest* of our profession, Christ Jesus; who was faithful to him who appointed him, as also Moses was faithful in all his house. For *this man* was accounted worthy of more glory than

Moses, inasmuch as he who hath builded the house hath more honor than the house. For every house is builded by some man ; *but he that built all things is God.*" (Chap. iii. 1-5.)

On the fifth, sixth, seventh and eighth verses of the second chapter, Paul declares that to angels "is given the government of the world to come ;" and to man, who was made but *little lower than the angels*, was consigned the government of the earth. All men, according to Paul, like Jesus, were born but little lower than the angels—and Christ by him is put on a level with all humanity. It is evident that the first chapter, as written by Paul, has been suppressed, and the one which has descended to us is made to take its place. It is not possible that Paul wrote the first and second chapters as they now stand. In the one case Christ is made *more* than the angels ; and in the other case he is made *less*. In the one case he is the *Creator* of the world, "*upholding all things by the word of his power ;*" in the other he is a High Priest of the order of Melchisedec, and one of the descendants of Abraham. In the first chap-

ter he formed the world, and in the third chapter it is said, " He who built all things is God."
The doctrines here declared are unreconcilable,
but it is not difficult to distinguish between
those of Paul and those of the men of the
second century.

Paul speaks of three orders of the priesthood :
that of Melchisedec, that under the Levitical
law, and that under the new covenant, with
Christ at the head.   What was the character of
the priesthood of the order of Melchisedec, Paul
does not say—nor do we know where to look
for information on the subject.   He was " without father, without mother, without descent,
having neither beginning of days, nor end of
life ; but made like *unto the Son of God :* abideth
a priest continually." (Chap. vii. 3.)   When we
are informed in the same chapter that Christ is
a priest after the order of Melchisedec, " who is
made, not after the *law of a carnal commandment*, but after the power of an endless life "
(ver. 16), we detect the insidious and subtle
poison of the Alexandrian school.

Here we have a Logos, who was in the beginning, and who would continue through all

time, which could never be true of any of the
descendants of Abraham. The priesthood under the Levitical law, Paul claimed, had
passed away, and was succeeded by a much
better one with Christ as its head. The last was
superior to the old because it would " continue
forever, an unchangeable priesthood." (Chap.
vii. 24.) In this new and better dispensation,
Christ is as superior to Moses and Aaron, as the
new covenant is superior to the old. Christ is
called a High Priest, " a minister of the sanctuary, and of the true tabernacle, which the Lord
pitched, and not man." (Chap. viii. 2.)

If Christ was the Son of God, born of a virgin,
when Paul was instructing his countrymen in
the mysteries of the new covenant, and was
pointing out to them the relation which Christ
bore to the same, as compared with Moses under the old, how happened it that he fails to
make mention of this important fact altogether ?
How can we account for the silence of Paul at
such a time on a subject of such vital importance ? He was a man of learning, and well
versed in all that was written by the Hebrew
prophets ; and if the fourteenth verse of the

seventh chapter of Isaiah had any application to Christ, or any other prophecy in the Old Testament, why did he not point them out to his countrymen, and in this way prove that Christ was not only superior to Moses, but to the angels?  Why call him a High Priest, and admit his Jewish descent, from the father of the Hebrew nation?  Who so well as Paul could define the *status* of Christ under the new covenant?  His numerous visits to Jerusalem, not long after Christ's death, his intimacy with all the disciples, gave him every and ample means for information ; and the deep interest he took in every particular which related to Christ stimulated inquiry ; and whatever he found that was important to be known as a part of the new faith, he would not fail to proclaim in tones of thunder, from the Euphrates to the Tiber.

We can well imagine his astonishment when the doctrines of the Greek school first began to make headway in his little churches.  We can form some idea of his feelings by reading the eleventh and twelfth chapters in the second epistle to the Corinthians : " Would to God ye could bear with me a little in my folly : and

indeed bear with me. For I am jealous over
you with godly jealousy : for I have espoused
you to one husband, that I may present you as
a chaste virgin to Christ. But I fear, lest by
any means, as the serpent beguiled Eve through
his subtilty, so your minds should be corrupted
from the simplicity that is in Christ. For if he
that cometh preacheth *another Jesus whom we
have not preachèd*, or if ye received another
spirit, which ye have not received, or another
gospel, which ye have not accepted, ye might
well bear with him." (2 *Cor.* xi. 1–4.) Rendered into plain language, he says : Would to
God you would pardon my zeal and anxiety on
your account. Having instructed you in the
religion of Christ, I am jealous and over-anx-
ious that you should stand as examples of pure
Christianity, and not surrender your pure and
virgin faith in Christ, carried away by the subtle doctrines of cunning men. If any one
speaks of Christ, and claims that he is anything different from what I have taught you—
or if any one has preached to you a different
religion or a different gospel, from that which
you learned of me, you show your forbearance

if you do not visit your anger upon them, who thus labor to mislead and deceive you.

Throughout these two chapters Paul shows deep sorrow on account of the progress of the new faith, and with his expressions of regret, he mingles words of reproof. The troubles growing out of it followed him through life. They harassed him in his prison. He lived to see all Asia turned away from him. With an aching heart he makes one last request of Timothy: "And the things that thou hast heard of me among many witnesses, the same commit thou to faithful men, who shall be able to teach others also." (2 *Tim.* ii. 2.)

15

# APPENDIX

## (A.)

FEW passages from history have given rise to more discussion than the following from Suetonius : " He," meaning the Emperor Claudius, " banished all the Jews, who were continually making disturbance, at the instigation of one Crestus." (*Life of Claudius*, sec. 25.)  The original is as follows : " *Judæos, impulsore Chresto, assidue tumultuantes, Roma expulit.*"  Does this order of banishment refer to the Christians ?  Dr. Lardner and others think not.  All difficulties vanish when we bear in mind, that the Christians then at Rome were Jewish converts from Judea.  The writer knew little about Christians, and knowing them to be Jews, he says all Jews were banished, which included the Jewish converts as well as those who opposed Christianity. All engaged in the riot were included, and none but Jews were. These Jews were constantly making disturbance at the instigation of one Crestus : that is, they were quarrelling about Crestus, which was a continual subject of quarrel among the converted and unconverted Jews everywhere. The writer knew so little about Christ that he failed to get the name correct, or there may have been a mistake on the part of the transcribers.

### (B.)

As a proof that the most learned scholars and correct thinkers, when under the influence of an early bias, are liable to the most gross mistakes and delusions, the following writers have given the authority of their names to the belief, that Peter uses the name Babylon in a figurative sense : Grotius, Macknight, Hale, Bishop Tomline, Whitby, and Lardner. But a large majority of writers hold to the literal meaning. Bishop Pearson, Le Clerk, and Mills think that Peter speaks of Babylon in Egypt. Beza, Erasmus, Drusius, Dr. Cave, Lightfoot, Basnage, Beausobre, Dr. Benson, A. Clarke think that Peter intended Babylon in Assyria ; Michaelis, that Babylon in Mesopotamia was meant. The frequent use of the word Babylon in the Revelation attributed to St. John, which there stands for Rome, is the principal argument used by those who contend for a figurative sense. This book is the most impious and malignant production among all the forgeries of the second century, and its design can be readily exposed, if it was worth the time to do it. Christ, whose last words were used in prayer for the forgiveness of his enemies, is made through St. John to pour forth feelings full of hatred against those who disagreed with the writer on matters of doctrine, especially the followers of Paul. He hurls his envenomed shaft at the heart of the great Apostle. It was at Ephesus where the war was warmest between Paul's friends and the followers of the Alexandrian school. To the church at that place, Christ is made to say : " I know thy works, and thy labor, and thy patience, and *how thou canst not bear them which are evil:* and thou hast tried them which say they are *Apostles, and are not, and hast found them liars."* (*Revelation* ii. 2.) Who could use such language but a malignant partisan? Christ, the Son of God, is made to use the language of a bar-room bully. When will those who profess to be Christians, learn that Christ was all kindness, gentleness, and love. They admit the authenticity and divine origin of writings that prove the Son of God was not even a gentleman.

### (C.)

THE writings ascribed to the Fathers, especially Polycarp and Ignatius, are entitled to little consideration; for nothing is clearer than that their names were used by the men of the second century to supply proof when disputes sprang up, or give authority to doctrines when divisions arose. The introduction to the epistle of Ignatius, addressed to the church at Rome, is a bare-faced attempt to prove that there was a church at Rome during the reign of Trajan, at the beginning of the second century. It was written not only to prove that there was a church at Rome at that time, but that it was the bank or depository of divine riches, "*wholly, filled with the grace of God, and entirely cleansed from any other doctrine.*" But we submit the whole passage to the judgment of the reader. "Ignatius, who is also called Theophorus, to the Church which hath obtained mercy in the majesty of the Most High Father, and his only Son Jesus Christ, beloved and illuminated through the will of him who willeth all things, which are according to the love of Jesus Christ, our God; (to the church) which presides also in the place of the region of the Romans, worthy of God, and of all honor and blessing and praise; worthy to receive that which she wishes, chaste, and pre-eminent in charity, bearing the name of Christ and of the Father, which I salute in the name of Jesus Christ, the Son of the Father: to those who are united both in flesh and spirit to all his commands, and wholly filled with the grace of God, and entirely cleansed from the stain of any other doctrine, be all undefiled joy in Jesus Christ our God."

The forger overdid the work in which he was engaged. This language, addressed to a church illuminated with all things according to the will of Christ and God, and worthy to receive all blessings and praise, proves that the passage was written at a time when the dogma of the Apostolic succession was in vogue, and Rome was putting forth claims to spiritual supremacy.* No time was more unpropitious to prove that there was *such a church* at Rome, than that

---

* The strong probability is, that the letter of Ignatius is a forgery throughout, and was gotten up for the sake of the *introduction*. Condemned ·by Trajan, and ordered to be carried to Rome to be devoured by wild beasts, for the amusement of the people, it is claimed the letter was written on his way to that city. Why he should write to the church at Rome while on his way there, is something remarkable, since there is nothing in the letter that was important to be known to the Christians, if there was any there, before his arrival. The epistle breathes a spirit which is unnatural and repugnant to every feeling of humanity. The following is a specimen of the whole. "May I enjoy the wild beasts which are prepared for me; and pray that they may be found ready for me: which I will even encourage to devour me all at once, and not fear to touch me, as they have some others. And if they refuse, and will not, I will compel them." (Sec. 5.) Why would Ignatius write an epistle of this character to the Romans while he was on the way to Rome himself? especially "as he was pressed by the soldiers to arrive at the great city before the public spectacle, that he might be delivered to the wild beasts." Why import a Christian Bishop from Antioch for the wild beasts of the Amphitheatre, if there was one to be

embraced in the reign of Trajan, when Christianity was a crime, which subjected the believer to the penalty of death. There being no Christians in Rome from the death of Paul to the time of Hadrian, it leaves the time to be taken up by traditions, which was gladly seized upon by Irenæus, who populated it with Bishops and others, the offspring of his own imagination.

## (D.)

WRITERS in the third and fourth centuries, for reasons sufficiently obvious, take pleasure in scandalizing the name of Domitian as the persecutor of Christians, and the great enemy of the Christian cause. It is claimed he put to death many persons accused of Atheism, the common charge against Christians, on account of their refusal to offer incense or to worship the ancient gods of Rome. Flavius Clemens, his cousin, is given as an instance. Now hear what a cotemporary historian has to say on the subject:

---

found in the mean time in Rome? Where was Clement, the third Bishop? Our confidence is not increased in the genuineness of this letter, that the first distinct reference is made to it by Irenæus.

15*

"Flavius Clemens, his cousin-german, a man contemptible for his indolence, whose sons, then of tender age, he had avowedly destined for his successor, and taking from them his former names, had ordered one to be called Vespasian, and the other Domitian, *he* suddenly put to death upon some slight suspicion, almost before the father was put out of his consulship." (Suet., *Life of Domitian*, sec. 15.) As the tyrant affected great reverence for the gods, he would not fail to visit the most severe punishment on those whom he judged guilty of irreverence, and as the Christians of that day were bold in the face of the most imminent danger, they could not escape the vengeance of the tyrant, had there been any in Rome upon whom he could lay his hands. With a disposition that was willing to furnish any number of victims, Eusebius has succeeded in giving the name of a single one. He says, "At the same time, for professing Christ, Flavius Domitilla, the niece of Flavius Clemens, one of the consuls of Rome at that time, was transported, with many others, to the Isle of Pontia." (Eus., *E. H.*, book iii. chap. 18.) The truthful father has succeeded in giving the name of one Christian who had suffered under the reign of Domitian, and that was a case of banishment.

As to the expression, '' and many others,'' it is only an easy way of conveying a falsehood without incurring the risk of detection. The story of John's banishment to the Isle of Patmos, like everything else which relates to this Apostle, is founded on a *tradition* of the third century, and is unworthy of serious notice. The story told by Hegesippus, of the treatment received by the grandchildren of Jude, called the brother of Jesus, at the hands of Domitian, if entitled to any credit at all, only goes to refute the charges made against him. As the story runs, these children were brought before him on the charge of being Christians. After hearing what they had to say, '' Domitian dismissed them—made no reply—but treating them with contempt as simpletons, commanded them to be dismissed, and, by a decree, ordered the persecution to cease. Thus delivered, they ruled the churches, both as witnesses and relations of the Lord. Such is the statement of Hegesippus,'' says Eusebius (book iii. chap. 20).

Here is a clear case for persecution ; but proceedings are dismissed, and those who were the objects of it treated with contempt.

Suetonius makes special mention of the persecution of the Jews under the reign of Domitian, who was governed, in their case, by his love of money rather than his regard for the cause of religion. The vast amount of money expended by him in the erection of palaces and public edifices had ruined his finances, which he undertook to relieve by the confiscation of the large estates and wealth in the hands of this people. To his rapacity there was no limit in such cases, short of the ruin of his victims. It is in vain to attempt to relieve the memory of the son of Vespasian and brother of Titus from the ignominy of the most odious and detestable crimes. From Augustus to Trajan, no one who bore the name of emperor is more justly entitled to the name of monster. He put to death his own cousin, Flavius Sabinus, because, upon his being chosen at the consular election to that office, the public crier had, by a blunder, declared him to the people—not consul, but emperor. Virtue as well as vice stood in awe in his presence.

The genius and learning of Tacitus and Pliny made it unsafe for them to remain in Rome, and both avoided danger by seeking obscurity. But to his other crimes are not to be added the murder of Christians, who were wise and cautious enough to avoid his presence.

The following dates are assigned to the epistles of Paul by Dr. Lardner and others :—

| EPISTLES. | PLACES. | A.D. |
|---|---|---|
| 1 Thessalonians | Corinth | 52 |
| 2 Thessalonians | Corinth | 52 |
| Galatians | Corinth | at the close of....52 or early in.......53 |
| 1 Corinthians | Ephesus | 57 |
| Romans | Corinth | about the end of..57 or the beginning of 58 |
| 2 Corinthians | Macedonia (perhaps from Philippi), | 58 |
| Ephesians | Rome | 61 |
| Philippians | Rome | before the end of..62 or the beginning of 63 |
| Colossians | Rome | 62 |
| Philemon | Rome | about the end of..62 or early in........63 |
| Hebrews | Italy (perhaps from Rome), | about the end of..62 or early in....,...63 |
| 1 Timothy | Macedonia | 64 |
| Titus | Macedonia | 64 |
| 2 Timothy | Rome | 65 |

www.ingramcontent.com/pod-product-compliance
Lightning Source LLC
Chambersburg PA
CBHW031127120726
47905CB00006B/1592